"In recent months I've often needed to work so late I've found it easier to stay over at the office."

"Oh." Ariadne seized on the potential escape hatch and said eagerly, "Well, if you'd rather do that tonight, don't you worry about me. I can look after myself."

Sebastian's brows shot up and his eyes gleamed. "But it's your wedding night, Ariadne."

She flashed him a brilliant smile. "I know—but, heavens, I'm not so hung up on all those old traditions. If you need to go somewhere and do things, go right ahead."

His brows drew together, and he said silkily, "There are *some* traditions that shouldn't be ignored."

As a child, **ANNA CLEARY** loved reading so much that during the midnight hours she was forced to read with a flashlight under the bedcovers, to lull the suspicions of her sleep-obsessed parents. From an early age she dreamed of writing her own books. She saw herself in a stone cottage by the sea, wearing a velvet smoking jacket and sipping sherry, like Somerset Maugham.

In real life she became a schoolteacher, and her greatest pleasure was teaching children to write beautiful stories.

A little while ago she and one of her friends made a pact to each write the first chapter of a romance novel in their holidays. From writing her very first line Anna was hooked, and she gave up teaching to become a full-time writer. She now lives in Queensland, with a deeply sensitive and intelligent cat. She prefers champagne to sherry, and loves music, books, four-legged people, trees, movies and restaurants.

# WEDDING NIGHT
# WITH A STRANGER
## ANNA CLEARY

~ CONVENIENTLY WEDDED...& BEDDED! ~

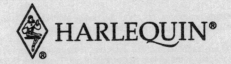

HARLEQUIN®

TORONTO • NEW YORK • LONDON
AMSTERDAM • PARIS • SYDNEY • HAMBURG
STOCKHOLM • ATHENS • TOKYO • MILAN • MADRID
PRAGUE • WARSAW • BUDAPEST • AUCKLAND

Recycling programs
for this product may
not exist in your area.

ISBN-13: 978-0-373-52780-9

WEDDING NIGHT WITH A STRANGER

First North American Publication 2010.

Copyright © 2010 by Anna Cleary.

# WEDDING NIGHT
# WITH A STRANGER

# CHAPTER ONE

ARIADNE leaned over the balcony rail and contemplated plunging into the sea. Serve Sebastian Nikosto right if she was found floating face down. He'd have to look elsewhere for a bride. But though summer heat shimmered on the afternoon air, Sydney Harbour looked deep and chill, and she edged back. Knowing her parents had died in those restless waters didn't make them any more appealing. She could be eaten by sharks!

The view was spectacular, she supposed, even after the heart-stopping beauty of Naxos, but it all felt remote to her. Her joy in coming back to Australia had withered. She felt as alien as she ever had in any foreign place. Incredible to think she was born here.

She turned back into her hotel suite and sank onto the bed's luxurious coverlet, reaching listlessly for the tour brochure that had sucked her in. The Katherine Gorge. Uluru. How thrilled she'd been, how excited. The sad joke was there never had been any such pleasures intended for her. She was here to be chained to the bed of a stranger.

Unless she ran. The minuscule hope reared again in her heart. This Sebastian Nikosto had failed to meet her plane. Maybe he'd changed his mind?

The phone rang and she nearly jumped out of her skin. Thea, ringing to apologise for the trick and tell her to come home? Explain about the mistake with the hotel booking?

It was Reception. 'Good afternoon, Miss Giorgias, you have a visitor. A Mr Nikosto. Do you wish to meet him in the lobby, or shall I give him your room number?'

*'No.'* Her heart had jolted out of its niche but she gasped, 'I'll come down.'

With a shaking hand she replaced the phone. She would just have to tell Nikosto she was Ariadne Giorgias, an Australian citizen, not a commodity to be traded in some deal.

She struggled on with her jacket. Her face was paler than her blonde hair, her eyes the dark blue they looked when she was angry, or afraid.

Her legs felt numb. On the way down in the lift she tried to quell her nerves with some positive thinking. Courage was all that was needed. Australia was a civilised country. Women couldn't be forced here. In fact, she was curious to see what sort of man would sink so low as to barter for a wife in the twenty-first century. Was he so old he was locked in the traditions of the past? So repulsive as to have no other choice?

Anyway, she was brave. She would refuse. After all, she was the notorious bride who'd left the heir to one of the richest fortunes in Greece standing at the altar. That had taken courage, though her uncle and aunt's world had judged it differently.

Still, when she stepped out of the lift on the ground floor and saw the obese elderly man in baggy clothes standing near the reception desk, she felt the blood drain from her heart. How could they? How *could* they? Then, even as the opulent lobby with its long low lounges and glass-walled views of the city swayed sickeningly in her sight, the man hailed some people across the room and walked to join them.

Oh. So not him. That small relief, at least. For the moment.

Her anxious gaze roved the groups of travellers, busy hotel staff, people queuing at the desks, and lighted on another unaccompanied man, this one tall and lean, dressed in a dark suit. He was standing by the entrance with his back to her, phone to his ear, jacket switched back at one side while his free hand rested on his hip. He was pacing backwards and forwards with a lithe, coiled energy, occasionally gesticulating with apparent impatience.

He turned suddenly in her direction, then checked. Her nerves jumped. She could tell he'd caught sight of her because the lines of his tall frame tensed, and even from this distance she could see him frown. He said something into his phone, then snapped it shut and slipped it inside his jacket.

Despite her moment of bravado, her stomach clenched.

He hesitated a moment, then walked across the wide lobby towards her, his frown smoothing away. Too late though, because she'd already seen it. As he drew nearer she saw, with a growing sense of unreality, that he was good-looking. A sleek, beautiful male in the matchless Greek style, though he had that indefinable, characteristic bearing of an Australian man. Athletically built, even in a suit. Why would he ever need to order in a woman?

He wasn't so old. Thirty-three or -four, nothing more than that. He might just be a nephew, or cousin. Perhaps she was mistaken, and he wasn't the one.

He halted at a couple of metres distance.

'You're Ariadne Giorgias?'

His voice was deep and beautiful, but it was his eyes that held her. They were mesmerising, a dark glinting chocolate fringed by thick black lashes. They swept over her in a cool assessment, made cooler by the stern set of his mouth, but she could guess what they sought. Her breasts, her legs, her child-bearing hips. Would she be a sufficient trophy?

She felt the proud colour rise to her cheeks. Anger and humiliation made her voice scrape in her throat. 'Yes. I'm Ariadne Giorgias. And you are…?'

Sebastian heard the stiff tone and his expectations received instant confirmation. So, Miss Ariadne Giorgias, child of the

Giorgias shipbuilding dynasty and his potential wife, was as spoiled as she was rich. Despite his fury at the trap he found himself in, he felt a curious edge of anticipation as he examined her face for the first time. Whatever transpired, this might be the woman he married.

Her face was nothing like the one he'd once thought the ultimate in feminine beauty, but he could concede it had a symmetry. He could imagine how his sisters would have described it. Heart-shaped, with those cheekbones.

She had creamy skin with an almost satin translucence, and quite astonishing deep blue eyes, glittering now with some sort of emotion. Her full mouth was especially sensuous, somewhere between sweet and sulky. An alluring blend of sultriness and innocence, if he could believe that. A siren's mouth.

She could have been worse. If a man was blackmailed into marriage, whatever the failings that had brought the woman to this point, she should at least look presentable.

He swept the rest of her with a judgemental gaze.

Her hair was a pale ash, paler than it had been in the photo the magnate had posted, though her dusky eyebrows and lashes gave away its true colour. He supposed she was beautiful, if a man happened to admire that particular style of beauty.

She was slightly smaller than he'd expected, though in her designer jeans and jacket her body appeared slim and, he had to admit, graceful, with pretty breasts, a waist so slender a man could span it with his hands, and sweetly flaring hips.

As far as he knew anything about women's apparel she was dressed well, nothing flamboyant. Limited jewellery, though what she had was no doubt the finest money could buy.

He realised his pulse was pumping a little faster than the average. All right, so she was attractive with those eyes. She could afford to be. She seemed pale, perhaps she was nervous, but he cut any softer emotions that might have evoked.

She *should* be nervous. She'd be even more nervous when she understood the sort of man she'd had the gall to attempt to add to her acquisitions.

As the full picture sank in he found his eyes needing to return to her face.

His lungs tightened. Yes, certainly, it could have been worse.

'Sebastian Nikosto,' he said finally, making a belated move to extend his hand.

Ariadne kept hers at her side. Never to touch him, she resolved fiercely. Not if she could help it.

His brows twitched, and she knew he'd taken note of her small rebuff. But he stayed as smooth as glass. 'Your uncle arranged that I should meet you and show you around Sydney.'

'Oh,' she said softly. 'So it was you who was to meet me at the airport?'

His eyes glinted, then were almost immediately screened by his thick black lashes. 'I apologise for not managing to be there. Tuesdays are always demanding for my office and I'm afraid I got caught up. Still…' He smiled, though it didn't reach his eyes. 'I guessed you would be quite experienced in these matters.' Somehow his voice was the more cutting for being so gentle. He spread his hands. 'And here you are. Safe and sound, after all.'

What 'matters'? With a pang she wondered what he'd heard about her. Would news of the wedding debacle have reached this distant shore? 'Experienced' was no innocuous word. Or did he assume she must be easy? Traded like a piece of livestock on a regular basis?

'No harm done,' he added.

Offhand, to say the least.

She thought of the morning she'd spent waiting for someone—*any* friendly face—at the airport, her agony of fear and indecision after the long trip and being tricked onto the plane. Praying that somehow, against all the odds, she'd misunderstood, and there *would* be a representative of the Nikosto family waiting with open arms to invite her into their warm family home. Worrying if she should take herself to the hotel, or run like the wind to some safe haven. Only what safe haven, when she was a stranger here?

The only vague knowledge she had of Australia, apart from her memories of her parents' home, remote flashes of that first little primary school, was the beach house her parents had taken her to for a visit with some distant relative of her mother's. She had no idea where it even was.

As an apology this didn't even rate. Had he been so reluctant to interrupt designing his satellites, or whatever he did? These days, did men expect their mail-order brides to deliver themselves to the door?

'I'm sorry you are dragged away from your work now,' she said, equally gentle. 'Perhaps you would prefer to postpone *this* meeting.'

One thick black brow elevated. 'Not at all, Miss Giorgias. I am charmed to meet you now.'

The words were smooth, but uttered in a silky tone that conveyed a wall of ice inside that elegant dark navy suit and pale blue shirt, colours that perfectly enhanced the bronzed tones in his skin and his blue-black hair.

Then, paradoxically, as if her coldness had somehow stirred the male in him, his dark eyes made an involuntary flicker to her mouth, hooked there an instant too long.

She angled a little away, her blood pulsing, indignation struggling with her body's involuntary response to the disturbance in the atmosphere surrounding his big masculine body. Testosterone, no doubt. It was only natural he'd be thinking about her in terms of sex.

She pulled the edges of her jacket a little closer. 'I'm not sure what my uncle told you, Mr Nikosto, but I came out here for a holiday. Nothing more than that.'

He considered her with an unreadable expression, then blasted any pretensions of innocence she might try to place on the situation.

'I'd have thought Pericles Giorgias would have been in a position to buy his niece a bridegroom from any of the grand houses in Europe, Ms Giorgias.' His eyes swept over her again in a smouldering acknowledgement of her desirability. 'I'm surprised to have been so—honoured. And flattered, of course.'

The words blistered her sensibilities. She saw his eyes flare with a dark, dangerous emotion that wasn't anything like feeling flattered, or honoured, and shock jolted through her. The man was angry. Was she such a disappointment? She didn't want him to want her, but the insult sank deep, just the same.

But she mustn't let him see her as some toothless lioness. He'd better learn she could defend herself.

'I'm surprised you *could* be bought, a man like you,' she mocked, though her voice trembled.

His eyes flashed. 'You'd better be sure you know what you've bargained for, Ms Giorgias. Tell me, once you have me shackled to your side, what do you hope to do with me then?'

She met his smouldering dark gaze, and tried to repress visions of lying naked beside him on some wide bed. Of being held in his arms, pressed against his lean, hard body, his dark eyes... But, she wouldn't... And he couldn't want to... She'd never...

She quickly thrust the images away. What could her uncle have promised on her behalf? With a helpless sense of shame, she scrambled to find some gloss to minimise the outrage Thio Peri had committed against her autonomy.

'My uncle arranged this holiday simply so we could meet. That was all. Just so we could—*meet*. To see if we... To see if there would be any...' She felt the hot tide of embarrassment rise through her chest and neck and all the way to her ears, and, furious at her weakness, added hoarsely, 'There is no requirement for—for anything further. I'm a free woman. This is the modern world.'

His chiselled, sexy mouth made a faint disbelieving curl, then he said very politely, 'Oh, right. Sure it is. But try to understand this, Miss Giorgias, I'm a serious guy. I'm not some racing-car celebrity or a prince with time on his hands between yacht races. I have a company to run. Some people choose to work, in case you haven't heard. I won't be able to devote myself to your entertainment twenty-four seven.'

He was so cold and unfriendly, all her hurt and tension, the fear and helplessness of the plane trip, the shock of the betrayal, wound her up to an emotional explosion. The fiery blood rushed to her head and she snapped, 'I'd rather you didn't devote yourself to me at all, Mr Nikosto.'

She felt the shock impact of her words, then all at once had a burning consciousness of his gaze on her clasped, trembling hands, and tried to shift them from view. Her loss of control had generated something, though, because she sensed a change in the air.

Sebastian stared, for the first time seeing the shadows under her fierce blue eyes, the rapid, vulnerable pulse in her tender throat. With a sudden lurch in his chest he had a flash of himself as a brute holding some delicate, threatened creature at bay.

A creature with sensitivities, nerves and anxieties. With soft silky breasts under her stiff little jacket. He couldn't control the overpowering thought. A creature—a *woman* who might soon be his to undress.

If he signed that contract.

Her sulky mouth made a tremor, and against his will, against all the odds, his blood stirred. Hell, but she had a kissable mouth. An intensely kissable mouth.

Poised on an emotional tightrope, her defensive instincts up in arms, Ariadne sensed the tension emanating from him rock into a different sort of beat.

He drew in closer, bringing her the faintest trace of some pleasant masculine cologne, and her sexual receptors suddenly roared into awareness of his big, vibrant body. Behind that blue shirt there was a beating heart, flesh, blood and raw, muscled power.

'Sebastian,' he stated. 'Look, er, Ariadne… It's all right if I call you Ariadne?'

She gave a jerky shrug.

'Whatever you choose to call your presence here, I've agreed to play my part in it. Unless you'd rather pass on the whole thing?' His expression was suddenly grim, his eyes hard and challenging.

It was an ultimatum. Her heart skipped an alarmed beat. What if he phoned her uncle and told him she was being uncooperative? After the plane trick, she wouldn't put it past Thio to refuse to help sort out the accommodation mix-up. It occurred to her then that the bungled hotel booking mightn't even be a mistake.

With limited money, and no way of paying for thirty nights at Sydney prices, she might very well be forced to beg for this man's generosity.

With a sinking heart she realised this could be exactly what they'd planned. Her uncle's words came back to her with a chilling significance.

'The Nikostos are good people,' Peri Giorgios had asserted before she'd woken up to his ploy. 'They'll look after you. I'm guessing they'll have you out of that hotel and into the Nikosto family villa in no time.'

The Nikosto family villa. Except it wasn't the Nikosto *family*. It was one member of it. One angry, ice-cold member.

Until she could talk to her uncle and aunt again, get a clearer idea of where she stood money-wise, perhaps her best option was to pretend to play along.

She met Sebastian Nikosto's dark eyes and crushed down her pride. 'No. No, look.' The words were as ashes on her tongue. 'I'm—really very grateful for your kindness.' Her voice cracked on the last one.

His heavy black lashes lowered. The faintest flush tinged his cheek as he said brusquely, 'All right, then. So—dinner this evening? I'll pick you up here at seven.' His eyes flickered to her mouth. 'Might as well—make a start.

# CHAPTER TWO

ARIADNE walked fast, up and down the hotel suite's sitting room until she'd nearly worn a furrow in the carpet. Then she strode furiously around straightening the pictures, shifting lamps to more pleasing positions, realigning the chairs.

Her uncle's scheme had placed her in an impossible situation with that icy, smouldering man. What had he been offered to marry her? No wonder he had such a low opinion of her, but why, oh, why had he agreed if it enraged him so much?

Maybe, if she could have despised *him* more, she wouldn't feel so ashamed. Ashamed of her uncle. Ashamed of herself and the mess she'd fallen into by thinking she was in love with that smooth-talking liar, Demetri Spiros.

Imagine if Sebastian Nikosto heard about the wedding scandal. Her uncle's words on the subject had rung in her ears all the way to Sydney. 'There isn't a man in Greece who would touch you now with a very long pole.'

Surely her uncle must know that if she did ever marry someone, even someone 'bought'—she flushed again in memory of Sebastian's stinging words—the man would have to be told about the scandal.

Other things Sebastian had said returned to her now with scathing significance. *Some people choose to work, in case you haven't heard.* As if he'd assumed she had no professional qualifications of her own. Did she look as if she'd spent her life as a useless ornament?

She kept rephrasing the things she'd said to him and turning them into what she should have said. Next time she saw him... Tonight, if she could bear to face him tonight, she'd set him straight about what sort of woman she was. And if he thought for a second, for an instant, that she would ever be available to him...

When the storm had calmed a little, she sat on the bed and forced herself to reason. In Athens it would be morning. Her uncle would be on his way to his office, her aunt engaged in either her beauty routine or instructing the housekeeper. Thea Leni was always affectionate and easy to deal with, though her compliance in the subterfuge to trick Ariadne onto the plane had been a painful shock. The hurt felt more savage every time she thought of it. Her loving aunt must have believed in her husband's solution to the 'Ariadne problem', at least a bit.

She put her head in her hands, still unable to believe all that had happened. Had they intended it as a punishment? She'd believed in their kindness absolutely, ever since, after the accident, they'd brought her as a seven-year-old to her uncle's house on Naxos. Though quite a lot older than her parents, they'd done all they could to replace them. In their old-fashioned way they'd loved her, protected her, even to the point of making her feel quite suffocated by the time she reached eighteen.

Why hadn't she woken up sooner to this holiday idea? When had Thio Peri ever wanted her to leave Greece without them in the past? Everything she'd done, every step she'd taken from the time she was seven, had been done under his care and protection, as if she were the most precious individual on the planet.

Even when they'd sent her to boarding school in England, either Thea Leni or Thio Pericles himself had come personally at every half-day and holiday to collect her. Long after she'd returned to Athens to attend university, she'd been told that one of the gardeners employed at the school had in reality been her own personal security guard. Thio Peri had never stopped worrying that she might be kidnapped and held to ransom.

How ironic. Once she'd been their jewel, but since she'd let them down and caused the scandal she must have lost her lustre. In their traditional way of thinking they still believed a large part of family honour depended on the marriages their sons and daughters made, the grandchildren they could boast of.

It wasn't too hard to understand. They'd never stopped grieving over their own childless state. They'd pinned all their hopes on her, their 'adopted' daughter, to provide the nearest thing to grandchildren they could ever achieve.

'You'll *like* the Nikostos,' Thio Peri had enthused on another occasion, determined to lure her into the trap. 'They're good people. They'll look after you. My father and old Sebastian talked in the taverna every night for fifty years. They were the best of good friends. You will be taken care of there every step of the way.'

Thea Leni had hugged her so tightly. She should have seen then that it all felt like goodbye. 'It will do you so much good, *toula*. It's time you visited your own country.'

'I thought Greece was my country now,' Ariadne had put in, grateful they were at last moving on after the months of recriminations. And, face it, a little nervous to be venturing so far on her own at long last.

'And so it is. But it's important to see the land of your birth. Admit it. You've lost your job, you've lost your flat, people are whispering about you… You need the break.'

*They* needed the break. She could see that now. From her. From the embarrassment she'd brought them.

It wasn't until she was on the plane buckling her seat belt that she'd woken up.

'Sebastian will meet you at the airport and show you around Sydney,' her aunt had said at the very last.

Her uncle's hearty laugh had followed her down the embarkation corridor. 'Don't come back without a ring on your finger and a man in your suitcase.'

She should certainly have known then. Sebastian's name had hardly been mentioned until that moment. Still, it wasn't until the hostess was preparing to embark on the safety rigmarole that a shattering possibility had dawned. In a sudden panic, Ariadne had whipped out her mobile and dialled.

'Thio. Oh, oh, Thio.' Her voice shaking with a fearful certainty. 'This isn't some sort of matchmaking thing, is it? I mean, you haven't set something up with this Sebastian Nikosto, have you?'

Guilt always made her uncle bluster. 'You should be grateful your aunt and I have taken matters into our hands for you, Ariadne.'

'What? How do you mean?'

His voice crackled down the phone. 'Sebastian Nikosto is a good person. A fine man.'

'*What?* No, no, Thio, no. You must be joking. You can't do this. This isn't my choice…'

'*Choice.*' His voice rose in her ear. 'You've had choices, and look what you did with them. *Look* at yourself. You're nearly twenty-four years old. There isn't a man in Greece—*Europe*—who will touch you. Now try to be a good girl and do the right thing. Be nice to Sebastian.'

'But I don't *know* him. And he's old. You said he was old. This is a *holiday.* You promised—you said—'

Her tearful protests were interrupted.

'Miss, miss.' The flight attendant was hovering over her, something about turning off her mobile phone.

'I can't,' she told the man. *She,* who had always hated a fuss and had turned herself inside out at times to avoid making trouble. 'Sorry,' she tried to explain to the anxious little guy. 'I have to…' She made a hurried gesture and turned back to the phone, her voice spiralling into a screech. '*Thio Peri*, this isn't *right*. You can't *do* this. This is against the *law*.' Her uncle hung up on her and she tried furiously to redial.

'Miss, please…' The attendant held out his hand for the phone, insistence in his tone. Her neighbours were staring with avid interest. All heads were turned her way.

'But this is an emergency,' she said. Glancing around, she realised the plane was already taxiing. She panicked. 'Oh, no, no. I have to get off.'

She dropped the phone, unbuckled her seat belt and tried to rise. Someone across the aisle dived for her phone.

The urgent voices. 'Miss, sit down. Miss. Sit, please. You are endangering the passengers.'

People around her stared as she half stood, clinging to the seat in front of her, craning their necks to see the distressed woman. Then the plane accelerated for lift-off, and she plumped down involuntarily. She felt the wheels leave the ground, the air under the wings, and was flooded with despair. They would have to turn back. The pilot would have to be told.

When the white rooftops of Athens were falling away below two more attendants had arrived, concerned and more authoritative. 'Is anything wrong, Miss Giorgias? Are you ill?'

'It's my—my uncle. He…' Already they were out over the sea and heading up through clouds. 'We have to go back. There's been a mistake. Can you please tell the pilot?'

She took in their bemused expressions, the quick exchange of glances, and lurid images of the headlines flashed through her head. *Ariadne Giorgias provokes airbus incident. Ariadne of Naxos in more trouble.*

More scandal, more shame. More mockery of her name, using the coincidence of the ancient myth. She cringed from the thought of any further notoriety.

In the end she fastened her seat belt and apologised.

But she couldn't just acquiesce. She might be stranded in a

hotel room, in a strange city on the other side of the world with no one to turn to except a man who despised her, but she mustn't give into panic. She had to keep her wits about her and find a solution.

First, though, she needed to be practical. She had expected many of her meals and all of her accommodation to have been paid in advance for the coming weeks, and her bank account was virtually empty except for the holiday money. Money for a little shopping, taxis, tips, day trips here and there. Holiday money. What a cruel laugh that was.

She took a deep, bracing breath and dialled Thea Leni's private line at the Athens town house. This time she mustn't lose control, as she had with the call from the plane.

'Eleni Giorgias?'

Her aunt's voice brought Ariadne a rush of emotion, but she controlled it. Thea sounded wary. Expecting the call, Ariadne guessed.

'Thea. It's me.'

'Oh, *toula,* don't… Don't… Your uncle has arranged everything and it will be good. You will see. Are you…all right?'

Ariadne's heart panged at the note of concern but she made herself ignore it. This wasn't the time for tears. 'There's been a mistake in the hotel booking,' she said in a low, rapid voice. 'I find that I'm only booked for one night, and it hasn't been paid for. The travel agent must have made an error. And when I met the tour director in the lobby my name wasn't on his list. I thought Thio had paid in advance. And he was supposed to have paid the hotel for four weeks.'

There was a shocked silence. Then her aunt said, 'Not paid for? But—but how…?' Then her voice brightened. 'Oh, I know what he's thinking. Consider, *toula,* you won't *need* to be in that hotel for long.'

The ruthlessness of the trick stabbed at Ariadne. Whatever had happened to chastity before marriage? 'Oh, Thea, what are you asking me to *do*?' This time there was no controlling her wail of anguish. 'Are you expecting me to go straight into that man's bed?'

Guilt, or perhaps shame, made her aunt's voice shrill. 'I'm not asking you to do anything except to give Sebastian a chance. He is a good man. He will marry you. He is rich, he has brains… Your uncle says he is a genius at what he does with the satellites.'

'He doesn't *want* to, Aunt. He doesn't want to marry me.' She wound up to a higher pitch. 'I'm not even cut out to be a wife.'

A gasp came down the line loud and clear, all the way from Athens. 'Never *say* that, Ariadne.' Her aunt was shocked to the foundations. 'Where is your gratitude?' she wailed. 'You had a bridegroom who *was* willing and you stood him up at the altar rails and dishonoured the entire Giorgias and Spiros families. Your uncle's oldest *friends*.'

Emotion welled up in Ariadne's throat. She understood. After they'd taken so much care to keep her pure for her husband, in the eyes of their traditional world she'd been deflowered, dishonoured, and still had no husband to show for it. And what else was a woman for, in her aunt's old-fashioned view, except to be a wife and mother?

'I told you, Thea. He was unfaithful. You know it. He had a lover.'

Even from a hemisphere away she could hear her aunt's world-weary sigh. 'Oh, grow up, Ariadne. If you want to bear children you have to compromise, and put up with—things. Anyway, there is no use in all this arguing. Your uncle won't change his mind.'

'He has made a mistake, Aunt. This man won't take an unwilling wife. If you met him you'd know. He's not… He's an Australian. He will walk away. Could you please…please, Thea, transfer enough money into my account for the hotel bill?'

She could hear tears in her aunt's voice. '*Toula,* if it were up to me…of course I would. Listen, when you're married all your money will be settled on you. Your uncle loves you. He thinks this is right. He only wants the best for you.'

'He always thinks he knows best, and this *isn't* best,' she said fiercely. 'And I won't do it. Tell him there's no way anyone will force Sebastian Nikosto to go through with marrying an unwilling woman.'

Her aunt was silent for a second. Then she said in a dry voice, 'Oh, yes, he will. He certainly will go through with it. As I understand it, there's nothing he wants more.'

'What are you saying?' Ariadne said, seized by an icy foreboding. 'Why do you think that?'

'Oh…' Her aunt's voice sounded weary, more distant somehow. 'You know I don't know about business, Ariadne. Your uncle says Sebastian knows he has everything to gain from this marriage, and everything to lose if he doesn't choose it. His company will fail if he doesn't marry you. Celestrial. Isn't that what it's called?'

Sebastian rang the bell of his parents' house, then strode straight in. He should have been back in his office, combing through the departments for more ways to cut costs to avoid cutting people, but events had wrenched his unwilling attention in another direction.

Before he took another false step, he needed to do some research. There had to be some explanation of why he of all the eligible Greeks on the planet had been chosen as bridegroom to the niece of Peri Giorgias.

When Giorgias had thrown in that extra clause at the time the contract was all but finalised, the completed designs on the table, at first it had seemed nothing more than a bizarre joke. The cunning old fox had chosen his moment well. With Celestrial suddenly adrift in the recession, the market dwindling, the sly operator must have known if he pulled out then, Celestrial would make a significant loss in terms of the precious resources already used to develop the bid.

In the gut-wrenching moment when Sebastian had understood that the eccentric old magnate's demand was deadly serious, he was faced with a grim choice. Accept the woman and save his company, guarantee the livelihoods of his workforce, or walk away and face the possible ruin of all he'd built.

But why him? Why not some rich lothario back in Hellas?

Angelika, his mother, and Danae, his married sister, were ensconced in the kitchen, arguing with the cook over the best method of preparing some delicacy. Angelika interrupted her tirade with hugs, and a multitude of solicitous enquiries concerning his diet and sleep patterns. Danae listened to all of it with an amused expression and an occasional solemn nod.

Sebastian shot his sister a glance. She might have been amused, but he was willing to bet she was soaking up the technique so she'd know how to suffocate her own sons when the time came for them to escape from her control.

'Look at how *thin* you are,' his mother wailed like a Greek mother. 'What you need is a really good dinner. Maria, set him a place. I have a moussaka in the fridge I was saving for tomorrow's lunch, but this is the bigger emergency. Danae, put it in a box and he can take it home with him. Show that woman how to feed a man.'

He held up his hand. 'No, thanks, Maria.' A really good dinner was his mother's inevitable cure for any disorder from flu to insomnia. 'I'm not staying.' He waved away the proffered dish. 'Put it back. I do have a full-time housekeeper, you know. And Agnes is very touchy about her cooking.'

His mother snorted her contempt. 'Cooking? *What* cooking? The trouble with you, my son, you are too wrapped up in your satellites to see what's in front of your nose.'

His nephews caught sight of him then and came running with a thousand urgent things they needed to tell him at once.

Sebastian listened as patiently as time would allow to all the recent details of their exuberant young lives, while Danae looked on, beaming with maternal pride.

Eventually, he detached himself with a laugh. 'That's enough,' he said, ruffling the two four-year-old heads. He waited for a brief respite in the voluble trio of voices, then jumped in with a query of his own. 'Is Yiayia here?'

His mother tilted her head in the direction of the hall. 'In the orangery.'

Sebastian approached quietly, in case his grandmother was having a late afternoon nap. He needn't have been concerned.

Dressed in her gardening smock, her hair coiled loosely into a bun, the small, frail woman was up and active, struggling to lift a terracotta pot onto a bench.

'None of that,' Sebastian said, striding forward and removing it from her worn hands. 'You know what the doctor said, Yiayia.'

'Oh, pouf. Doctors,' his grandmother exclaimed while Sebastian positioned the pot in the miniature rainforest that was her pride and joy, adorning every available space. 'What do they know?'

She peeled off her gloves and reached up, tilting her soft, lined cheek for his kiss.

Sebastian obliged, declining to argue, knowing she worshipped the members of the medical profession as though their words were piped direct from heaven.

'Well, *glikia-mou*. Now, what are you about?' She settled herself into a high-backed wicker chair draped with shawls, while Sebastian sat facing her.

Filtered by leaves both inside and out, the afternoon sun slanted through the glass walls, bathing the room in a greenish light.

Sebastian made himself relax, aware he was being examined by an almost supernaturally astute observer of human frailty. 'Do you remember the Giorgias family?'

Her elderly brows lifted. 'From Naxos?' He nodded, and she said, 'Of course. From when I was a child. There was always a Giorgias in our house. My father and their father were friends.'

'Do you remember Pericles Giorgias?'

'Ah.' She gave a sage nod. 'Of course I remember him. He was the one who inherited the shipyard, and the boats. He married Eleni Kyriades. He was such a generous man. It was he who helped your father when the stores nearly collapsed back in the eighties.'

Sebastian tensed. 'How do you mean, he helped Papa? Are you sure?'

'For sure I'm sure. When the banks wouldn't help Pericles made your father a loan. To be repaid without interest over a very long time. No strings attached.' She shook her head in wonderment. 'Such a rare thing, generosity.'

Dismay speared through Sebastian. Such generosity was rare indeed. But there'd been strings attached, all right. Strings of honour. With grim comprehension he recognised the situation. The Nikostos were now under an obligation to the Giorgiases. For some reason Peri Giorgias required a favour, and he'd chosen to collect from the son of his debtor.

A son for a father. A favour for a favour.

He could almost hear the clang as the trap snapped shut around him. Chained to a stranger in wedlock.

In an attempt to break free from the vice sinking its teeth into his gut, he got up and paced the room. Another marriage was the last thing he'd ever intended. How could he dishonour Esther's memory with some spoiled tycoon's poppet?

'There were other brothers too. Three. At least three.' Yiayia's gentle voice filtered through his reflections. 'I remember the youngest, but the middle boys…' The old lady sat back in her chair and closed her eyes. After a moment she said, 'I remember young Andreas. He didn't care for the family business. I think he was an artist. He came out here, and married an Australian girl. Oh, that was a terrible tragedy. Poor Andreas and his wife.'

In spite of his resistance to knowing anything about the Giorgias woman's history, Sebastian's attention was arrested, and he turned to watch his grandmother's face. 'What happened?'

'A boat accident. Night-time on the harbour. You may not remember. Your parents, your grandfather and me, we all went to the funeral, but you'd have still been a boy. Only imagine a Greek being killed in a boating accident! They said it was a collision. Silly young people out skylarking. Andreas and his wife didn't stand a chance.'

He frowned, unwilling to feel sympathy. Unwilling to feel. 'They left children?'

His grandmother's face lit up. 'That's right, there was a child. A girl, I think. I'm nearly sure the poor little thing was taken back to Greece with one of the brothers.'

Sebastian grimaced and resumed his chair. After a smouldering moment he made the curt acknowledgement, 'Pericles.'

'Ah.'

A pregnant silence fell.

Sebastian wondered if by admitting he knew that one fact, he'd given away something crucial. Sooner or later, if he went through with this charade, they would all have to know. What would they think of their brilliant son then, snagged like a greenhorn in a duty marriage? Forced up the aisle with a woman he hated?

A flash of the Giorgias woman's drawn, anxious face at the last stirred a sudden unaccountable turmoil in his chest and he had to rescind the thought. No, he didn't *hate* her, exactly. He just felt—angry. What man wouldn't? To have his bride, his *life*, decided by someone else.

In the first flush of his outrage Sebastian had blamed—he allowed himself to use her name—*Ariadne*. He'd imagined her as a spoiled little despot, winding her doting uncle around her little finger. How had she come to choose him? Had he been listed in some cheap catalogue of eligible males?

Now, after hearing Yiayia's words he began to see it was almost certainly instigated by Pericles himself.

His grandmother studied his face, her shrewd black eyes revealing nothing of her thoughts. After a long moment, she said, 'You have met her? Andreas's daughter?'

Sebastian hesitated, then shrugged and said without expression, 'I have had that pleasure.'

The wise old eyes scanned his a moment longer, then closed, as if in meditation. 'I don't think Pericles and Eleni were blessed.'

Sebastian knew what she meant. Other people might be blessed with brains, beauty, talent, health or wealth, but to Yiayia children were the most worthwhile of life's gifts, so blessings referred only to them.

'They'd have wanted to take on the little one,' she continued. 'I expect they'd have been overjoyed. Eleni had nothing much else to fill her heart. That Pericles liked the business. He was the right one to take over the shipping because he had an eye for money. Clever, but not always very smart. Andreas, now… A thoughtful boy, I think. Sensitive.' She shook her head and clasped her lined hands in her lap. 'Oh, that was a terrible shame. The young shouldn't have to die.'

Was she thinking of Esther now? 'No,' he said shortly. 'They shouldn't.'

Again, her wrinkled lids drifted shut. She remained silent for so long Sebastian thought she must have nodded off to sleep. He was about to get up and cover her with one of her shawls when her eyes opened, as clear and focused as ever.

'Is she beautiful?'

Sebastian's gut tightened. Resistance hardened in him to the notion of Ariadne Giorgias's beauty. He opened his mouth to growl something, but nothing would come. Anyway, the less said the better. Regardless of how he felt, whatever he said now could come back to haunt him.

'Do women have to be beautiful, Yiayia?' he hedged. 'Wasn't there an entire generation of women who rebelled against that notion?'

The old lady made an amused grimace. 'They usually are, though, aren't they, *glikia-mou?* To the men who love them. A man needs something lovely to rest his eyes on.'

Again, he guessed she was thinking of Esther. And it was true he'd loved her as much as it was possible for a man to love a woman. People in his family rarely made reference to her now, not wanting to remind him of the bad times, all the losing battles with hope after each bout of surgery, the radiation treatment, the nightmare of chemo.

Even after three years they were still exquisitely careful of his feelings, even Yiayia, tiptoeing around him on the subject, as if his marriage were a sacred area too painful for human footsteps.

Sometimes he wished they could forget about all that and remember his wife as the person she'd been. He still liked to think of those easy-going, happy days, before he and Esther were married, before he'd started Celestrial.

A stab of the old remorse speared through him. If only he'd spared her more of his time. In those early days of the company...

With an effort he thrust aside the useless self-recrimination, thoughts that still had the power to gut him. Too late for regrets, now he'd lost her.

No one would ever replace her in his heart, but often he was conscious of a hollowness that his work, exciting and challenging as it was, didn't fill. He hardly spent any time at home now, even sleeping on the settee in his office at times. He could imagine his parents' amazement if he ended up marrying this Greek woman, after they'd long since given up hope and become inured to the prospect of his ongoing singularity.

The reality was, he might as well admit it, one way or another a man still needed a woman. Somehow, against his will, against all that he held decent, meeting Ariadne Giorgias in the flesh had roused that sleeping dragon in him.

Though she wasn't his choice, she was no less lovely than any of the women he knew. If he'd met her at some other point in time, he might even have felt attracted. But...

Resistance clenched inside him like a fist. He wasn't the man to be coerced.

He became aware of Yiayia's thoughtful scrutiny. What was it she'd asked? Beautiful. Was she?

'She probably is,' he conceded drily. 'To anyone who cares for her type.'

'What type is that?' Yiayia enquired.

Defensive, scared, fragile. Pretty. Sexy.

# CHAPTER THREE

MIDWAY through winding her hair into a coil, Ariadne's hand stilled. What had Sebastian Nikosto meant by 'a start'? And how much of a start? Surely he wouldn't expect to kiss her. Or *worse*.

She remembered his cool, masculine mouth, the seductive blue-black shadow on his handsome jaw, and felt a rush in her blood. Panic, that was what it must have been, combined with a fiery inner disturbance to do with how little she'd eaten since she'd boarded the plane.

The man had revealed himself as a barracuda. Her feminine instincts told her he might want to try something, but she'd just have to hold him off. That shouldn't be so hard, given how much he'd disliked her at first sight.

She'd managed to hold Demetri at bay for months, even though they'd been engaged and she'd believed herself in love. She made a wry grimace at herself. What a fool she'd been.

Afterwards, Thea had hinted that that might have been where she'd gone wrong with her ex-fiancé, but Ariadne knew better. It was *because* he'd had the mistress that Demetri hadn't been concerned about making love to her.

And everyone knew that like or dislike didn't necessarily have much to do with a man's sexual desires. Take Demetri's case. He'd made love to people he didn't even *know*. And she'd been such a contemptible pushover, believing his lies every time, doubting the evidence her close friends had tried to give her. Making excuses for his lack of interest in her, because she'd wanted to believe it was all fine and everything was as it appeared. Until she'd gone for lunch at that Athens restaurant and seen him there with his girlfriend.

It had still taken her days to accept the reality, but she'd never be so naive again.

It would hardly make sense if Sebastian Nikosto wanted to kiss her, after the things he'd said, but nothing about this whole situation made sense. The more she puzzled over it, the more her confusion increased.

She felt as if she were locked in a nightmare. If only she could fall asleep she might wake up and find herself back in her bedroom in Naxos. Had Sebastian's anger been with her, or with the deal he'd struck with her uncle? He'd made it sound as if the whole thing had been her idea.

Some aspects were so ironic, she'd have laughed if she hadn't been in such distress.

Thio had probably thought she would suit an Australian Greek because of her Australian mother. Meanwhile, Sebastian Nikosto had taken one glance at her from across a room and had felt cheated. She'd never forget that frown, how it had speared through her like a red-hot needle.

Was it because she wasn't attractive enough? Had her uncle explained to him that the woman he was throwing in to sweeten his pillow had blue eyes, *not* the dark shining beautiful eyes most Greek women took for granted as their heritage?

She stabbed a pin into her chignon. Whatever happened, she would die before she kissed a man who'd been paid to take her. No wonder he judged her with contempt. She must seem like the leftovers on the bargain rack in the Easter sales, thrown in as an added incentive. She was almost looking forward to meeting the man again and showing him his mistake. She truly was.

Despite all her bravado, the coward inside her was tempted not to keep the dinner engagement. What if she were to lie low in her room with a headache instead? In the morning, simply check out of the hotel and disappear from Nikosto's life without a trace?

She would have to check out, anyway. She wasn't sure what the price would be, but with the grand piano and all in the suite she guessed she wouldn't be able to afford many nights here.

After the devastating conversation with Thea, desperation had inspired her with a survival plan. If she sold what little jewellery she'd brought and added the proceeds to her holiday money, provided she found somewhere cheaper to stay, she should have enough to get by on until she could find some sort of job. There must be art galleries in Australia. Under the terms of her father's will, unless she married first she couldn't inherit her money until she was twenty-five. All she had to do was to stay alive another fourteen months.

More and more throughout the afternoon her thoughts had returned to that beach house on the coast. She wondered if her mother's auntie still lived there. Would she remember the little girl who'd come to stay nearly twenty years ago? Would she even be alive?

It was tempting to just cut all communication with Sebastian Nikosto and his accomplices in the crime *right now*. That was what the man deserved. What they all deserved, she thought fiercely. She should just vanish into thin air. Trouble was, if she did that he might raise some sort of alarm. She shuddered to think of how it would be if she were pursued by the Australian police. She could imagine the sneering headlines back in Greece.

*Ariadne of Naxos goes missing in Australia. Has Ariadne been eaten by crocodiles?*

*Ariadne, lost in the outback.*

And one that made her wince. *The runaway bride runs again.*

No, disappearing without saying goodbye could not be an

option. And there was no one else who could fix her dilemma for her. She was on her own, in a strange country, and for the first time in her life there was no one else to rely on except herself and her own ingenuity.

She needed to go downstairs in that lift, face Sebastian Nikosto squarely, and tell him eye to eye that she would never marry him, under any circumstances, and that she never wanted to see him again.

A surge of nervous excitement flooded her veins. What if he was furious? She almost hoped he was. It would do her heart good to see him lose his cool control and spit with rage.

She highlighted her cheekbones with liberal application of blush, at the same time boosting her mental courage with some strong, healthy anger. Whatever he said to her this time, however cold and hostile he was, whatever bitter insults he fired at her in that silky voice, there was no way her pride could ever let him think she was afraid of him.

Let the barracuda do his worst. Make-up would be her shield.

She painted a generous swathe of eyeshadow across her lids. Even without it her eyes had appeared dark and stormy after the adrenaline-wired past thirty-six hours. Now they looked enormous, and with more adrenaline pumping into her bloodstream every second there was no disguising their feverish glitter. She smoothed some kohl underneath with her fingertip. Somehow the blue of her irises deepened.

The effect was atmospheric, almost gothic, and intensely satisfying. She felt as if she were in disguise. What to wear was more of a worry.

She hardly wanted to inflame the man's desires. A burkha would have been her choice if she'd had one to hand, but pride wouldn't allow her to appear like a woman in a state of panic, anyway. In the end she chose a black, heavily embroidered lace dress that glittered with the occasional sequin when she moved. Since the dress had only thin straps she added a feathery bolero to cover her shoulders. The lining ended a few inches short of the hem, revealing a see-through glimpse of thigh in certain lights, but with the feathers added she looked modest enough.

At last, dressed and ready for battle, her breathing nearly as fast as her galloping pulse rate, she surveyed her reflection.

Red lipstick, the only touch of colour. Black dress, feathers, purse. The sheerest of dusk-coloured silk stockings, and black, very high heels to lend her some much-needed height.

All black.

Well, he wanted his Greek woman, didn't he?

Sebastian shaved with care, keeping an eye on the clock. Not that he felt any guilt over failing to meet the plane from Athens. Not exactly.

He was a busy guy. If he didn't keep an eye on Celestrial, who knew how much of a tangle things could get into? He could hardly place himself at the beck and call of every heiress with a whim to make him her husband.

Still, manners dictated that tonight he should make the effort to be punctual. It didn't have to be a late evening. He could buy her a decent dinner, smooth over the jagged hostilities of the first meeting, and be away by nine to get in some work.

He hoped Miss Giorgias was in a better frame of mind. She'd have been jet-lagged, of course, which would explain her waspish behaviour.

He splashed his face with water and reached for a towel, avoiding meeting his gaze in the mirror. He hadn't really been so hard on her, had he? There was a lot more he could have said. Anyway, hadn't she thanked him at the end for being kind?

He felt that uncomfortable twinge again and brushed it aside. For God's sake, did he have to be a nursemaid simply because he'd agreed—*under duress*—to meet the woman and check out the possibilities?

He dried off his chest, dropped the towel into the hamper, then slapped on a little of the aftershave his sisters had given him. Lemon, sage and sandalwood, the label read. *Guaranteed.*

He made a rueful grimace. Guaranteed to soothe a princess?

As rarely happened to a man with his gaze fixed firmly on the stars, his eye fell on a green, moss-like growth around the base of the tap. How long had that been there? It was robust enough to have established quite a hold. Agnes must have missed it. More than once, by the look.

He supposed he could attend to it himself without threatening his gonads. He cast about for something to wipe it away with, and used the only thing readily available: one of yesterday's socks. The sock made no appreciable difference, so he gave up.

With grander things to attend to, how could a guy be expected to attend to the demeaning sludge of housework?

He frowned into his wardrobe, then surrendered to necessity and chose an evening suit. Was the shirt clean? He checked that it had a recent laundry ticket attached. Lucky he'd remembered at some stage to remind Agnes to empty the washing hamper. It was only to be expected she'd forget things when he was hardly ever here.

Scrubbed, dressed and polished, he gave his overall appearance a cursory check. Looked at from a certain point of view, he supposed, the Giorgias woman had flown across the globe to nail him. *Meet* him, in her words. Might as well grit his teeth and make an effort to show her a little respect.

He was, after all, he supposed, an eligible guy. A single guy. *Widower.* He flinched inwardly as the loathsome word surfaced from the deep to strike him down with all its connotations of dust and ashes, funerals and long black days and nights that rang with emptiness.

He wiped those horrors from his mind and walked downstairs, a single man free and unencumbered.

At the hotel he tossed the car keys to the parking valet, then strolled into the lobby, conscious, despite everything, of a certain buzz of anticipation in his veins.

It was the hush of the evening, the city poised to leap into its nightlife, with neon lighting its every billboard and high-rise. Wherever he looked people were hurrying off to their evening engagements: guys with their girlfriends, couples holding hands. For once he felt like a man with somewhere to go other than the office.

Ms Ariadne Giorgias would've had an hour or two to rest, so hopefully she might be less prickly. He wondered what she'd be wearing. Something slinky? Some little designer number from one of the couture houses, exhibiting more skin than fabric?

The lobby was busy, but there was no sign of her. After his lapse this morning he would hardly be surprised if she kept him waiting as a punishment.

He strolled over to Reception and asked one of the clerks to phone up to her room.

The clerk had scarcely lifted the phone before Sebastian saw her. She was emerging from the lift along with some other people, but he singled her out at once. Unaccountably his lungs seized. Even after one brief meeting, he recognised the characteristic way she held herself. She walked with her head high, as though to ensnare every available ray of light in her hair, her slender, shapely body graceful and erect. He must certainly have been too long without a woman, because he found his gaze riveted to the sway of her feminine hips, and felt stirred at some deeply visceral level.

Whatever else she was, she was all woman.

The rushing sensation in his blood heightened.

She caught sight of him and her steps made an involuntary halt, then picked up again, and she advanced to meet him, her expression now cool and wary. That tiny, undeniable falter, though, resounded through him and struck his guilty heart like a blow.

A man didn't have to be an aeronautical design genius to see that underneath the fantastic black dress, slim shapely legs and silky gleaming hair, Ms Ariadne Giorgias was scared. He suffered a jolting moment of self-insight.

Was this what he had become? A cold, angry man who frightened women?

Conscious of her nervous pulse, Ariadne steeled herself to the challenge, then plunged onwards. Sebastian Nikosto looked more handsome, if possible, in an evening suit with a charcoal shirt and a bronze-hued silk tie that found golden glimmers in the depths of his dark eyes. She conceded reluctantly that his colours were again excellent, though the tie was slightly skewed as if he hadn't given it a final check.

Perhaps it was her imagination, but did his expression seem friendlier? Less—hostile?

His dark gaze swept her, and again she felt that roaring sensation, almost like excitement. There was a look in his eyes that made her too aware of her curves and the shortness of the dress. A million wild thoughts assailed her at the same time. Why, oh, why hadn't she worn trousers?

While her fingers nearly succumbed to a mad itch to tweak that tie into place, her pulse was thudding in her ears so loudly she hardly took in what he said.

'…Ariadne.' The way he said her name made it sound as if it had been wrapped in dark chocolate. One of those liqueurs they gave you with coffee at the Litse in Athens.

'Cheri Suisse.' Her voice sounded overly husky. Oh, *Theos*, had she actually said that? Surely not. Where was the poise she so desperately needed?

It was another of those awkward moments when he would expect to clasp her hand, but this time he went one better. Before she could forestall it, he leaned forward and brushed her cheek with his lips.

It was so unexpected her heart nearly arrested. She felt the slight graze of his shadowed jaw on her skin, and the heady masculine scents, the powerful nearness of him swayed her senses.

Flustered, her cheek burning as if she'd been brushed with a flame, she had one coherent thought swirling over and over in her brain. Here was a man whose interest in her was purely financial. This wild fluttering inside, these uncontrollable sensations, needed to be crushed into extinction. *At once.*

'I'm thinking we won't go too far afield tonight, since you're probably jet-lagged,' he said, as smoothly as if he hadn't been insulting her only a few short hours previously. 'I know a little place not far from here. Do you like Italian?'

She drew a deep breath.

'Listen, Sebastian…' She raised her hands before her like a barricade. 'I don't want to marry you.' He blinked, and before he could reply she added, a tremor in her voice, 'So—so you might not wish to waste any more of your time. Thanks anyway for— for coming.'

'What?' He looked stunned.

'Yep, that's right.' Wound up and swept by a massive charge of adrenaline, she gave him a cool smile. 'As the song says, I'm holding out for the prince.'

Without waiting to watch him crumble into a heap of masculine rubble, she turned on her heel and swept towards the lifts, rather pleased with her exit line. Unfortunately for her grand moment, before she'd gone more than a couple of steps the persistent man recovered himself and caught up.

'Well, er—hang on there a second.' He moved around to block her path. He was shaking his head, amusement seeming now to have replaced his astonishment.

She had to wonder if he'd understood. Or was he so in need of the money, he felt driven to try some other way to talk her round?

'That's fine, Ariadne,' he said. 'That's just fine. But whether we marry each other or not, we still have to eat dinner, don't we?'

His lean handsome face broke into a smile that was far more dangerous than his earlier sternness and hostility. Charming little lines appeared like rays of warmth at the corners of his eyes and mouth, and crept insidiously through her defences to assault her too soft heart. Here she was, all geared to be brave, to foil his cold, cutting words with icy hauteur, and now he'd changed tack.

It was confusing. And unfair. She was so desperately in need of a friend, if she wasn't careful, before she knew it she'd be forgiving him. Complying. The very word evoked a shudder.

Thank goodness Demetri's legacy had died hard. She reminded herself that a man's smiles came easily, and this one could hardly wipe away the distress she'd gone through since she'd boarded that plane. She needed to be strong, and, after so much humiliation, true to herself.

'I'm not very hungry,' she asserted coolly. 'I'll be happy enough just to order room service. Anyway, it was—interesting, meeting you.'

'Oh.' Perhaps he'd picked up on the edge in her voice, because he dropped his gaze and his smile faded. When he glanced up again she saw remorse in his eyes. 'I deserve that. I know I wasn't very welcoming earlier. You'd had a long flight and I…' His deep voice was suddenly contrite. 'I'm pretty ashamed of how I spoke to you this afternoon. I'd like to apologise properly, and explain, if you'll give me the chance.'

His eyes had softened beneath his luxuriant black lashes to a rich, warm velvet. She had the ghost of an impression of what it might be like to be someone he admired. Someone he felt affectionate towards. He looked so sincere, her instincts, always weakly anxious to think the best of people, rushed to believe him.

She felt herself begin to melt, then just in time remembered all those occasions with Demetri and steeled her heart against him. Men could be such smooth liars. Especially if there was a financial incentive.

'Apology noted,' she said softly. 'Goodbye, Mr Nikosto. Some other time, perhaps.'

Like some other life. Some other universe.

'Oh, look, Ariadne… Are you sure I can't tempt you to a little taste of Sydney nightlife? You look amazing in that dress. It's a shame to waste it.' His dark eyes flickered over her, a sensual glow in their depths. 'We don't have to go far. As it happens, this hotel is said to have one of Sydney's finest seafood restaurants.' With a lean hand he indicated the other side of the lobby. 'Won't you let me at least buy you a glass of wine? Break the ice?'

An olive branch was so tempting. She'd never been the vengeful type. His mouth relaxed in a smile, its warmth reflected in his eyes. With his sexy, deep-timbred voice seeping into her tissues like an intoxicant, the man was a powerhouse of persuasion.

She lowered her lashes to avoid his mesmerising gaze, her pulse drumming. Shouldn't she have one drink with him? Even with the off-balance tie, he looked so darkly handsome in his evening suit. The beautiful cloth was so well cut, it enhanced his wide-shouldered, lean-hipped six-three to perfection. It was hard to imagine he was anything but what he appeared. Civilised, straight, honourable, decent…

Unfortunately, Thea's information about his company's need for a cash injection was still lodged in her oesophagus like a spike. The hurt pride and shame surrounding the notion of herself as a prize in a transaction welled inside her again.

'No, thanks,' she said hoarsely. 'I think I'd prefer to go to bed early and read up on Australia.'

Sebastian felt a spurt of good-humoured frustration. How far did a man have to grovel to lighten the mood of this difficult and, the more he saw of her, really quite desirable woman?

He drank her in, admiring her black dress. Wasn't it the classic dinner garb women wore? That feathery affair she'd added couldn't conceal the shape of her breasts, the pretty valley dividing them. It was hardly a dress to be lounging in.

Unless of course it was lounging on a man's bed, prior to being unzipped.

He had a sudden hot flash of smooth, satin breasts spilling into his hands, meltingly tender raspberries aching to be tasted, but he banished it. Still, the thought of them stayed there just below his awareness, like a wicked temptation, dreamed of but forbidden.

He cursed himself for having alienated her and making his situation more complicated than it needed to be. The irony wasn't lost on him. He was the one who was reluctant to be married. Who'd have thought he'd have to end up fighting to win his unwanted bride for even the smallest dinner engagement?

In every corner of his being, instincts of determination and masculine self-respect gathered in momentum and roused his red blood cells to the challenge. He was reminded of one of his more complex satellite projects. The harder it had been to resolve, the more fired up he'd been to conquer it.

Added to that, he had a vested interest here. If he didn't marry her, where did that leave his contract with Peri Giorgias? Now faced with the real danger of her slipping from his grasp, with a galvanising immediacy he suddenly realised how crucial it was for him to keep her. He could hardly expect to persuade her against her will, but his entire being grew charged with an urgency to win. This little tussle, at least.

'Read up on Australia?' he echoed, appealing to her with the rueful charm he'd known never to fail with women. 'You'd prefer that to sharing an excellent dinner with a guy whose only desire is to make amends?'

Her glittering blue gaze met his without wavering. 'Depends on the guy.'

Touché. The thrust was as unexpected as a punch in the gut.

'Oh,' he said, his insides reeling. 'Right.'

Ariadne sensed the impact of her words and knew they'd hit home. She tensed, waiting for some blistering response. To give the barracuda his due, he controlled whatever it might have been.

He merely nodded. 'Fine,' he said with a shrug. 'It's your call.'

His eyes gleamed and his mouth hardened to a straight, determined line, but he raised his hand in a cool farewell gesture, 'Enjoy your holiday, then, Miss Giorgias,' and walked away.

As Ariadne watched his rigid, retreating back the sudden relief from tension made her knees feel wobbly. She let out the breath she hadn't even realised she'd been holding. Spying a nearby ladies' room, she made for it, and pushed her way into the blessed sanctuary for a moment of private self-congratulation.

Her first triumph of the day. She leaned up against the washbasin console until her breathing calmed. In the mirror her eyes had a dark glitter, as though she'd been in a fight. In a way she had, she recognised, and she'd come off victorious.

He'd looked so shocked, as if he'd been savaged by a sheep. Serve him right for conniving with her uncle to snare her like a helpless little lamb. A fleeting image of the sincerity in his eyes when he apologised flashed into her mind, but she dismissed that.

*Let* him be sorry. Let him suffer.

For once she hadn't succumbed to a man's wiles. She'd carried out her plan, and felt better for it. Empowered. With relish, she watched herself in the mirror make a symbolic gesture of dusting off her hands.

Let Sebastian Nikosto know how it felt to be scorned.

Empowerment must have been good for the soul, because it no longer seemed necessary for her to spend the evening cowering in her room. In fact, her appetite came roaring back and she felt ravenous enough to eat a lion.

She swept from the washroom and sashayed in search of the restaurant. Guided by the chink of china and the unmistakable hum of a large number of people tucking in, she found the entrance without much trouble. She could hear the smoky voice of a singer performing some bluesy old love song, and delicious cooking smells wafted to her. Garlic, herbs and exotic spices mingled with the savoury aromas of char-grilling meats to taunt her empty stomach. All at once she felt nearly faint with hunger.

She approached the entrance, feeling glaringly conscious of not having an escort. At the host's desk she paused. 'Excuse me,' she said, lowering her voice to avoid attracting too much attention. 'A table for one, please.'

The portly head waiter raised close-set brown eyes to regard her, and arched his supercilious brows. 'Name?'

'Ariadne Giorgias.'

A subtle and strangely smug expression came over the man's face. 'Do you have a reservation, Miss Giorgias?'

'Well, no.' She smiled, and almost whispered, 'I'm a guest in the hotel. I didn't think a reservation would be required.'

'I think you will find, madam,' he said in crushing tones, making no effort to lower his voice to spare her embarrassment, 'that in the finer hotels with restaurants of renown, a reservation *is* required.'

She flushed. 'Oh. Sorry, I didn't realise. The finer hotels I've stayed in before haven't expected a reservation in their dining rooms.'

The man's sceptical gaze clashed with hers. 'And which hotels might they be, madam?'

'Well…' She thought back. 'There was the Ritz in Paris. And the one in London. And the Dorchester. I'm sure The Waldorf in New York was very welcoming…' Although, her uncle and aunt had been with her on those occasions. She supposed there wouldn't be many head waiters who would refuse Peri Giorgias a table. 'Oh, and there was the Gritti in Venice. Though I'm not so sure about that one now. Maybe we did have a reservation there.'

The man drew in a long breath and seemed to swell, while at the same time his lips thinned.

'Madam,' he stated, with austere emphasis, 'this is the *Park Hyatt* in *Sydney*. Our rules may differ from those of the less *moderne* northern hemisphere establishments, but they are crucial if our guests wish to experience the continuing superbness of our cuisine.' He gave her a moment to digest the information, then lowered his gaze and darted his plump fingers across the screen of his little computer, frowning and pursing his lips. 'As it happens, madam is fortunate in that we do have one remaining table.' He picked up a menu, tucked it under his capacious arm, and, pivoting on his heel, made a grand gesture. 'If madam would follow me.'

He raised his hand, and another waiter materialised from somewhere, bearing a water carafe and a basket of freshly baked bread. Thankful for her stroke of luck in not being turned away, Ariadne followed the procession across the crowded room. Through the glass walls she received an impression of the harbour lights, vessels on the dark water, the hard glitter of the city rising up behind Circular Quay. The pale shells of the Opera House floated in luminous majesty, seemingly a stone's throw from the terrace.

As she threaded her way among the tables, she couldn't help noticing the small, delicious-looking morsels on the diners' over-large plates, and wondered anxiously if she should order double of everything.

She rounded a pillar after her guides and stopped short. Tucked into a corner between pillars and the step down to the terrace, was a small, round, vacant table, gorgeous with crystal, roses and pink and white linen. Right next to it, in fact, practically jammed against it, was another table, similarly adorned. Only this one wasn't vacant.

To her intense shock, lounging back in its single chair, his long legs stretched casually before him, Sebastian Nikosto sat perusing a leather-bound menu.

The host pulled out her chair and waited. Sebastian glanced casually up at her from beneath his black brows. His eyes lit with a curious gleam, then he resumed brooding over his menu.

Momentarily thrown, but loath to betray it or start a distressing scene, she hesitated, then submitted herself to be seated. With chagrin she noticed that her chair was positioned to face Sebastian's.

The head waiter deposited her napkin on her lap and presented her with her menu, while the other waiter fluttered to fill her water glass, offer her hot rolls.

She barely knew what she said to them. Questions clamoured in her head as Sebastian's dark satanic presence dominated the space. Had the man somehow guessed she'd be coming here after all and arranged this with the restaurant staff?

But how could he have known? Did he have some sort of diabolical clairvoyance?

The head waiter retreated, along with his small entourage. Almost at once a wine waiter advanced, who hovered, exerting polite pressure for her to make a choice. Conscious that this was something she'd never had to do herself before, she opened the wine menu and skimmed page after page of unfamiliar Australian and New Zealand names, hypersensitive to the unnerving presence of her neighbour.

She could feel his eyes on her, boring into her brain as if he knew, damn him, how distracting his presence was, how little she really knew about wine. Out of cowardice she considered rejecting it altogether, then noticed a bottle of red on the neighbouring table, its cork removed.

Allowing the wine to breathe, her uncle would have pronounced with approval.

Pride and prudence warred in her chest, and pride won the day. If Sebastian Nikosto could order wine, so could Ariadne Giorgias.

Still, she'd hardly ever been the person at the restaurant table who'd made the selection, except on a couple of lunch occasions with her girlfriends. Praying she didn't make a fool of herself, she murmured the most familiar name on the list.

The waiter's brows rose. 'Veuve Cliquot. Excellent choice, miss.'

The man whisked away, and she was left to face Sebastian alone. She held her menu up before her face, self-consciously aware he was now leaning forward with his arms folded on the table, watching her like a cougar poised to spring.

She felt a spurt of annoyance. His firm, masculine mouth—on another man she might have even considered it stirring—was gravely set, but there'd been a very slight flicker in one corner as if a smile was willing to break out. Except there was nothing to smile at. For goodness' sake, the man had just been rejected in marriage. Couldn't he accept it with dignity?

She was just winding up to say something to challenge him, when the waiter came back with a champagne flute, and presented a bottle with a yellow label for her approval.

As she'd seen her uncle do countless times, she nodded. The man set the glass before her, then without spilling a drop worked off the cork with deft fingers, and poured her a foaming taste.

As coolly as possible, considering she was under scrutiny, she swirled it in the glass, sniffed it, then took a small sip.

The buoyant liquid foamed its way to her stomach like a potent wave.

'Thank you,' she said, her eyes watering a little as the waiter topped up her glass. To crush any suspicions Sebastian Nikosto might have that she wasn't completely at ease and self-assured, she raised the sparkling liquid casually to her lips for a further sip. Bubbles shot up her nose and she couldn't prevent a sneeze. In the desperate grab for tissues, she reached blindly for her purse and accidentally knocked over her water glass.

*Oh, Theos.* A flood the size of Niagara Falls swamped her side of the table.

The waiter snapped into emergency mode, fussing over the pool with a napkin, helping her move out from the table to avoid the drips, enquiring if she was all right, if there was anything wrong with the champagne, trying to insist despite her protests that he must summon someone to change the table linen.

*Shut up,* she wanted to scream, burningly aware of Sebastian Nikosto's attentive face observing and listening to it all. *Get lost.*

'No, no, it's all *right,*' she hissed at all his mopping and tsking over the sodden spot. 'It's nothing. *Nothing.* I like it damp. Please,' she added with a heartfelt tug at his sleeve.

At last the guy took the hint, though unhappily, and edged away, casting uncomfortable looks back at her over his shoulder. The sheer irony of it, she kept thinking. Fate was so unfair. After her extensive experience in the grand restaurants of Europe, to appear now in her own country in front of the most unpleasant man she'd ever met as a gauche, clumsy fool was too much.

As soon as the waiter was out of earshot and she'd recovered some of her poise, Sebastian Nikosto drawled, 'Celebrating?'

She gave him a withering glance. There was an unnerving glimmer in his dark eyes, while that suspicion of a smile still lurked at the corners of his sexy mouth. He might not have personally upset the glass, but in her heart she blamed him. It was his fault for flustering her.

'That's none of your concern.'

At least her dress was black, she reflected. No one else had to know how uncomfortable she felt sitting with a wet tablecloth in her lap.

He leaned back in his chair and stretched with luxurious ease. 'Are you usually this snotty and touchy, Ms Giorgias?'

She drew a sharp breath and retorted, 'Are you usually this rude and annoying?'

He lifted his brows. 'Now, how fair is that? Here I am, a harmless guy, rejected by my date and forced to a lonely dinner, when by the most astonishing coincidence…'

She leaned forward. '*Is* it a coincidence?'

He narrowed his eyes thoughtfully. 'You know, just what I was wondering. I don't usually believe in coincidences. When you showed up here I was—have to admit it—gobsmacked. I have to wonder how it was arranged. It looks like a set-up to me.'

He made a sweeping gesture around at the setting. 'Here we are, in our own little intimate space, night-lights out there on the harbour, soft music, the terrace…'

She gasped. 'What are you implying? That *I* set this up?' She glared at his solemn face. 'That's ridiculous. I didn't know you were here. Why would I?'

He shrugged, shaking his head. 'Can't work it out. Unless you followed me because you felt—ashamed.'

'Oh, *what*?' she said incredulously. She rolled her eyes. '*I* should feel ashamed!' She glowered at him, remembering the way he'd behaved at their first meeting, even if he had made an apology since. 'Anyway, it wasn't a date.' She leaned forward again and added softly and distinctly, 'For your information, I wouldn't go anywhere with a man who had to use a business deal to catch a wife.'

His eyes glinted. 'Wouldn't you? But you'd come halfway across the world to meet him.'

The silky insinuation jabbed her and she retorted hotly, 'No, I would not, not if I had any—'

She pulled herself up in the nick of time. For all that her aunt and uncle had hurt and betrayed her into getting on that plane with their cruel trick, they were still her family. Still all the people she had in the world, though she could never forgive them. There was no way she could admit to Sebastian how cheaply they must have held her in their hearts all these years, even though she'd never before questioned their unconditional love for her.

His eyes sharpened. 'Not if you had any what?'

For the thousandth time that day she felt tears prick at the backs of her eyes. Blinking fast, she lowered them and turned away and pretended to look for something in her purse until the danger passed.

When she looked up Sebastian Nikosto's alert, intelligent gaze was still fixed interrogatively on her face. 'You were saying…?'

'Nothing,' she said huskily, grateful that food waiters chose that moment to swish up to each of their tables to take their orders.

Relieved that Sebastian's attention was diverted from her for the moment, she turned her attention to the menu and the efficient young waitress.

Since during her perusal she hadn't managed to take in a word of the menu, apart from one heartening glimpse of the dessert list, it took her a few moments to read it.

By the time she'd made up her mind, Sebastian had finished ordering his, and his waiter had hurried away. He lounged back in his chair, his long legs stretched out in idle relaxation. Though his gaze only drifted her way intermittently, she could sense his full attention trained on her like a million-megawatt spotlight.

With her cheeks growing uncomfortably hot, in the effort to exclude him she kept her voice at a low murmur. 'I might start with one or two chocolate truffles, and then the basil bruschetta.'

The woman looked surprised. 'The chocolate truffles are a dessert, miss.'

'Of course. I *know* that. Only one, then. And then could you cut me a really, really thin slice of that ricotta tart with the truffled peaches? Followed by the linguini...'

'Which one, miss? The broccoli or the prawn?'

She hesitated, weighing it up, then mumbled so softly the waitress had to bend her head to hear, 'Could I try a small taste of each? And I'll have the flounder with the artichoke and caper sauce.'

'That is a *whole* flounder,' a deep voice interjected from the other side of the neighbouring table.

Ariadne felt a sharp stab of annoyance. The man must have had supersonic hearing. Not to mention an insufferable nerve. As if he hadn't spoken, she kept her eyes firmly on the face of the waitress and murmured, 'And a garden salad to go with that, please. And vegetables.'

'Anything else, madam? Pommes Paris? Witlof gorgonzola salad with pancetta and Granny Smith apple?'

'Yes, yes, everything.' Ariadne leaned her head away from the direction of the Nikosto table and whispered, hoping the waitress would get the message and lower her voice as well. She smiled meaningfully at the young woman, wishing with all her heart that Sebastian Nikosto would implode and disappear. 'One more thing,' she said, barely moving her mouth.

The waitress tilted her head to catch her words. 'Yes, miss?'

Ariadne beckoned until the woman leaned her ear closer. 'I'm finding that the light is shining in my eyes here. Would you mind helping me to shift around to that side of the table?'

She could see it would be a squeeze, but it would have the advantage of her sitting with her back to Sebastian.

The woman eyed the space doubtfully. 'I'm not sure your chair will fit on this side, miss. It might be an obstruction when we try to serve the gentleman.'

The deep smooth voice intruded again. 'What if the young lady moves over here?'

Ariadne allowed herself a freezing glance at him.

He was indicating the space beside him, his dark eyes agleam, his smile exuding innocence and goodwill. 'Then she'd be facing away from the light, and she'd be able to enjoy the view. Since we're practically dinner partners already…' His eyes dwelled on Ariadne's face with a sensual, velvet intensity. 'I'd love to have you join me, Miss Giorgias.' His voice was awash with sincerity. 'And you'd be rescued from that wet tablecloth.'

The waitress's eyes warmed when she saw Sebastian. 'Oh, do you know each other?'

'God, yes,' he said heartily. 'Our families have known each other for ever, haven't they, Ariadne?'

Turning to Ariadne, the waitress caught sight of her tablecloth and her drooly expression changed to horror. 'Miss,' she exclaimed, 'this cloth is *soaked*.' She tested the sodden patch. 'Oh. You should have said. This table will have to be reset.'

She swivelled about, and had begun telegraphing across the room for reinforcements when Sebastian murmured something to her and pointed towards the lights.

Easily distracted if the distraction happened to be lean, dark-eyed with stunning cheekbones and a sexy, mocking mouth, the waitress turned to Ariadne, her eyes alight with meaning. 'What do you think, miss? Wouldn't you like to move?' With a lilt of her brows she indicated Sebastian. 'You shouldn't be bothered by the light over there.'

Ariadne was cornered in more ways than one, and her simmering gaze met Sebastian Nikosto's with sardonic appreciation. She wasn't sure how many of the staff he'd bribed, but that smile was anything but innocent. A refusal would make her look downright nasty, her request to move petty and insincere.

'Do you always have to have your own way?'

'I find it best.'

She glowered at him. 'Your tie's crooked.'

'Is it?' He smiled, as if he knew, damn him, how handsome it made him. 'Why don't you come over here and fix it for me?'

She folded her arms across her chest. 'I think you must enjoy punishment. I've already rejected you once this evening.'

His eyes glinted. 'You could always change your mind, though. I'm willing to bet you're pretty good at that.'

Her guilty past rushed to the surface. 'Why? What have you heard?'

His brows lifted with amused curiosity. 'What should I have heard? See? We're already talking. You might as well come on over.' He patted the spot next to him.

She exhaled a long, incredulous breath. Couldn't this man take no for an answer? On the other hand, her tablecloth was wet. And it couldn't hurt just to eat dinner with him, could it? He wasn't likely to whisk her away to his fortress and force her into a wedding ceremony at gunpoint in the dead of night.

'Oh, all *right,*' she said. 'Anything for peace.' The concession was barely wrung from her before Sebastian sprang up and, with help from the waitress, whisked her, her chair and place setting to the Nikosto table.

'There, isn't that better?' His eyes gleamed. 'Now we won't have to shout at each other to be heard.'

'I never shout,' she said coldly.

'No, and you never smile. I'm looking forward to removing that sulky expression.'

She smiled at him just to prove he was wrong, but, after all the horrors of the day, somehow the criticism wounded her already abused feelings. She clung to the smile as tightly as she could, her gaze fixed on a ferry chugging across the harbour in a blaze of lights while she fought the fatal thickening in her throat.

The silence grew charged. After a long tense minute he said gently, 'Ah… Now that I think about it, it might just be the shape of your lips.' He leaned closer and traced the outline of her lips with one lean finger, not quite touching them. 'They have that little pout. And they're very sensuous.'

His voice soaked through her nerve fibres like *kitro.*

# CHAPTER FOUR

DINNER had a dizzily mounting tension, not unlike a ritual dance in which each move and countermove weren't known in advance, but had to be guessed at by the dancers.

Ariadne felt weird to be dining with a man she'd so recently refused in marriage, but probably as part of some diabolical master plan Sebastian made no reference to it at all. He drew her along in conversation, smoothly and skilfully, even warmly, though not about the sensitive issues between them. He just skirted the edges of those. *Flirted* the edges. Despite the chilly start, the temperature managed to pick itself up off the floor.

Still, the subject lurked in every glance and nuance of the conversation. What sort of man persisted in charming a woman after he'd been rejected so finally and utterly? Shouldn't he have slunk off into the night? Perhaps he was hoping to change her mind.

And he did have charm. With every comforting mouthful of the heavenly Hyatt food, she felt increasingly aware she didn't dislike him as violently as she'd at first thought. Perhaps he wasn't a barracuda. More a smooth, sleek stingray with a devastating five o'clock shadow. And midnight satin eyes that made her pulse quicken. And a mouth to ravish a woman's dreams.

Her conscience wasn't quite at ease with the new situation, but she quelled it by thinking of it as an emergency. Now she was cast adrift upon the world, for the moment this small table, in this pool of light, with this smoothly determined, dangerous and— she had to admit—extremely attractive man, was all she had to cling to.

It was risky though, feeling this rocky and emotional in the presence of a handsome man and a bottle of champagne. Heartsore, tired people with jet lag could easily switch from sexy enchanting laughter to tears. To prove it, there was a small jazz band across the room, and a singer with a voice like dark honey plucked at her heartstrings with every line of every plaintive old love ballad she sang. *Cry me a river*, she sobbed. *Willow weep for me.*

The setting might have been exciting, and picturesque, with the constantly changing light show on the harbour as traffic streamed across the bridge, and ferries chugged in and out of the Quay lit up like Christmas, but she didn't feel she belonged. She felt so out of place, it was no wonder she was finding solace in the company of her despised bridegroom. *Aspiring* bridegroom.

Every so often she reminded herself this was her country too, but had trouble convincing herself.

She withdrew her gaze from the harbour lights to contemplate Sebastian. If he was regretting transferring her to his table, he wasn't showing it.

His sexy mouth was grave, but there was an unsettling warmth in his dark eyes whenever they rested on her, making her insides curl over with an exhilarating suspense. Meeting his eyes ran her the risk of being scorched. She knew she was flirting with danger, yet she couldn't seem to resist it.

And what with the warm summer air floating in from the terrace, she was getting overheated. 'It's hot in here,' she breathed to Sebastian. 'Don't you feel hot?' She took off her feathery wrap and draped it over the back of her chair.

When she did that an appreciative gleam lit his eyes that made her conscious of having crossed some sort of safety line.

His glance made the skin of her chest and shoulders tingle and burn as if razed by a solar flare. Call her a needy tart, but the sensation felt thrilling to a woman that no man in Greece— probably *Europe*—would touch, even with a very long pole.

Her sexual receptors were madly spinning. He would touch her if he got the chance, she felt sure.

'You set this up, didn't you?' she challenged him, caressing the stem of her glass.

He smiled in acknowledgement. 'I've never really liked eating alone.'

She glowered at him, hoping he didn't guess how seriously that sexy smile was seeping into her bloodstream and melting her resistance. 'How did you know I would be coming to the restaurant?'

He considered her, his sensual gaze flickering with masculine expertise from her face and hair, down her throat to her breasts. 'You've put your hair up. And the dress. You went to so much trouble to look gorgeous, I couldn't see you wasting it all in your room. Even to spite me.' Amusement warmed his eyes.

'Oh.' She flushed. 'Well, I hope it cost you heaps.'

Sebastian watched the delicate tide suffuse her neck, then rise to her soft cheeks, and felt a dangerous surge in his blood. The knowledge that he had the power to evoke such a response was seductive, to say the least.

He restrained his eyes from wandering to her breasts, though he was aware of them with every fibre of his being.

Now the thaw had set in, there was a sparkle in her blue eyes, brought about by the champagne, or the electric charge pulsing between them, he wasn't sure which. Either way, tonight his edgy bride had shown him alluring glimpses of her true self. Bubbly, mischievous, funny, though every so often he heard the tip of some other emotion tinge her voice. Sometimes her smile had a feverish quality, as if her mood could be fragile. Or was she excited?

His *supposed* bride, he corrected himself, watching her lips close over the chocolate-laden spoon while her lashes drifted down in utter bliss.

Disturbed from her appreciation of the divine chocolate by that searing gaze, Ariadne looked at him. 'Do you ever accept a no?'

The sensual flicker in the dark depths of his eyes triggered an answering response deep in her insides. 'Depends who it's from. And how much I want to get to know them.'

'You didn't want to get to know me this morning. Or this afternoon.'

'That was before I met you.'

'Am I supposed to be flattered?'

He considered her. 'Not flattered. Just alive to the possibilities.'

What possibilities? The word floated in her mind like a scintillating mist. Truth to tell, part of her had been alive to some possibilities since the moment she'd rounded that pillar and seen him occupying the table. Or maybe even before then. Perhaps from the first time his eyes had connected with hers across the lobby this evening and started her heart hammering.

She risked a gulp of her champagne, knowing very well it could be a mistake. The stuff was already effervescing in her veins, and she needed to keep her head.

But it was magic, frothing away her misery and easing her anxiety, or at least changing its flavour. Now she felt like a beautiful, desirable woman riding a wild and fantastic whirlwind, and if it wasn't the champagne making her feel that way, what was it?

As if to heighten her turmoil, the singer wrapped them in a smoky embrace with a nostalgic lament for a lost past in some shining place.

She was used to good-looking men with dark eyes and gleaming white smiles, but Sebastian had another dimension that could cut straight through her defences if she didn't take care. Though tonight he was subtly flirtatious, every so often that serious, steel quality shone through. Like her first impression, but without the anger and the ice.

She risked another glance at him. Definitely, the ice had melted, but he was a different species from Demetri and friends, strutting the playgrounds of the world with their lazy, sophisticated boredom. If she hadn't known the truth, she couldn't have imagined he'd have accepted a bribe to marry her.

What had he been offered? she wondered. Shares in the Giorgias line, with the expectation of his wife being heiress to the lot?

She pushed the horrid thought away and concentrated on the positives. She was, in fact, feeling better after the bruschetta, the sliver of tart, the two delicious serves of linguini, the fish—not that she'd eaten very much of anything. She was in far too much of an uproar. The chocolate pudding had been certainly beneficial, although there was also that glass of champagne. Or had it been two? There was the one she'd had before she'd moved...

She peered over at the ice bucket and tried to see how much was left in the bottle. Whatever the level, it had shored up her spirits and helped her to feel warm and glowing and alive, even a bit reckless.

'So what are you doing here with me?' she challenged, fluttering her lashes. 'Is there a shortage of women in Sydney?'

'Not that I've noticed. What's your excuse?' he retorted. 'Are the guys in Greece all doddery and near-sighted?'

She hesitated, evading his smiling, but still penetrating glance, regretting laying herself open to that painful subject. This was a murky alleyway she didn't want to venture down. The last thing she wanted to admit to him was that she'd exhausted her options in Greece. She didn't doubt her uncle's declaration for a minute. No Greek man would risk engaging himself to her now. Not after Demetri's experience and all the publicity.

She said huskily, 'I don't plan to get married. Ever. In Greece or anywhere else.'

'What if you meet someone you fall in love with?'

She shot him a sardonic look. The sheer irony of *him*, of all people, talking about love. 'Are you kidding?'

His brows lifted and she said, waving her fork, 'Let me try to explain, though like all men I expect you'll scoff.' Ignoring his blink, she wrinkled her brow in concentration, and tried to bring it down to words of few syllables. 'You see, my problem is I'd need the person to be in love with me as well. So we would be equals. How can you make promises and accept the blessing of the church without sincerity on both sides?' She looked earnestly at him. 'Do you think you can try to understand that concept, Sebastian?'

His eyes glinted, but she went on, regardless. 'That's why I can never risk it. You imagine someone loves you, then you find out they only wanted to marry you because they mistakenly thought you would inherit the Giorgias shipping fortune.'

His tanned, lean hands stilled. He'd understood that bit all right.

'So you aren't set to inherit?' He scanned her face with an alert gaze.

She might have predicted his interest, but still she felt a stab of disappointment. Just when she was thinking he might be different from Demetri.

He'd made his own feelings on the issue so clear this afternoon, it made her wonder, if he *was* hoping to talk her round, what sort of marriage had he in mind? A marriage in name only, where they signed the register then went their separate ways?

Oh, it was all so humiliating. Did greed always have to outweigh honour and integrity in every man alive? She let out a frustrated sigh. She should let him know right now his chances of using her to improve his fortunes were zilch.

'I won't get a cent of it, as far as I know,' she informed him, watching his face while she dashed his hopes. 'I have older cousins, all male, and the company will go to them. Thio Peri doesn't believe a woman can manage a business. Well, he knows, of course, women can manage *some*, but he doesn't think a woman could manage *his* business.' She sat back in her chair to await results. Would he rise from the table, bid her goodnight and disappear into the distance? 'I'm only a niece, you see. And besides, Thio knows I don't want to have anything to do with it.' With a bittersweet smile she added softly, 'The only thing I'm set to inherit is a little bit of money my parents left. They weren't rich, I'm afraid. We lived in a modest little cottage. I don't think they even owned it. So you'd have nothing to gain.'

He was silent for several seconds, his eyes downcast, his lean face inscrutable. Then he looked up at her. His dark shimmering eyes meshed with hers, deep and unreadable.

'If I married you.'

'That's right. If you… But you can't now, can you? Now that I've—refused you.'

He continued to hold her in his veiled gaze. The moment stretched, while her heart thumped and questions clamoured in her brain. What was he thinking? She had no real idea what her uncle had offered him, what he'd said. Had her warning been enough to put him off? Did he think he could change her mind?

Was she really so innocent? Sebastian wondered. It sounded as if she had no idea of the means her uncle had used to bring him to this point. If she had been set to inherit everything, he felt sure the old magnate would have had no hesitation about dangling his empire before his eyes. The fact that Pericles had never mentioned it to him made her claim seem likely to be true. In a strange way, it even made the outrageous deal slightly more palatable.

He grimaced. He must be going insane. What was wrong with him that made him find something to prefer in being blackmailed in a business deal over being bought like a stud stallion?

The dessert courses were cleared, and he watched her lift her head and turn a little to ask the waiter to pass on to the chef her undying gratitude for the chocolate pudding. The line of her cheek and neck, the smooth curve of her shoulder riveted his gaze and sank into his awareness like a hypnotic. Desire quickened in his blood.

Yiayia was right. He'd been without something lovely to look at for too long.

Even her voice, low and sweet, fell on his ears like an intoxication. Supposing he did decide to marry her, how hard would it be to persuade her?

'Nothing else for me, thank you. Sebastian?' She turned enquiringly to him. 'Cognac?'

He pulled himself together and waved away the menu, asking for the bill, only part of his mind engaged.

The rest of it was imagining how it might be to have Ariadne Giorgias as his wife. To meet those luminous blue eyes, that luscious mouth across his breakfast table. To bury his face in the silken mass of her hair and fan it across his pillow. To plunge himself into the slick heat of her gorgeous body and possess her utterly, until she cried out in ecstasy, night after night after long, hot night.

He drew a long breath and smiled. 'Do you feel like stretching your legs?'

Ariadne looked up, met his darkly handsome face and her heart skittered. Was this where he made his pitch? She hesitated. She could excuse herself, say goodnight, goodbye, and flee to her room. It flashed in on her then though, that once she was alone in her room, she'd have to face the cold reality that this would be her last night's sleep in safety and comfort. All she'd have to look forward to when she lay her head on the pillow would be the morning—homeless, and on her own resources in a strange country.

That morning was racing towards her like a black horror. She felt a deep dread, like an offender staring prison in the face for the first time. With a little shiver, she rose from the table.

The terrace hugged the hotel like the deck of an ocean liner, the sea lapping at its sides. In one direction Circular Quay was a blaze of activity, while far and wide lights twinkled all around the foreshore. As she gazed across at the opera house, its luminous pale shells rendered magical by moonlight, Ariadne could almost have believed she was on one of her uncle's cruise ships, heading for some romantic destination.

Perhaps she wouldn't mind living here, once she'd settled with a job and a place to live. Once she got over the hurt.

They moved out of the spill of light from the restaurant, and she felt grateful for the shadows, not having to keep her smile on.

She could sense a tension in Sebastian, too. The intensity of the mood had ratcheted up to a higher gear, as if the looming goodbye had brought her uncle's deal back to scream silently between them. The suspense that he was about to ask her to reconsider marrying him kept her nerves jangling.

As they strolled the terrace, though, chatting about tastes in books and music, he didn't mention it, or touch her. Maybe she was being super-sensitive, but it seemed to her he tried extra hard not to let his hand or any part of his clothing brush hers.

Like Demetri, only not like Demetri. With Demetri, she'd never had this taut, smouldering awareness. Never felt so feminine and desirable.

Sebastian eyed her profile and wondered what devil had tempted him to suggest strolling out here in the dark. As soon as he had her away from the crowd, it was hard not to think about her breasts, and how long it had been since he'd kissed a woman.

It must have been the power of suggestion. If it had never been suggested to him that she could be his, he probably wouldn't need to keep looking at her. He wouldn't be itching to smooth his hand over her shoulder, or be so achingly aware of the creamy rises swelling the black fabric of the dress. And there was the explosive fact lurking in the nether regions of his mind that she had a room upstairs, and a bed.

His loins stirred and he willed his flesh not to react to his luscious imaginings any further. She was so slender and petite, he had to wonder if she'd be large enough to take him.

He sighed. As if she'd read his mind she sent him a quick, searching glance, and he made a resolute attempt to keep the conversation on the straight and narrow.

'Do you remember much about Australia?' he said.

She looked up. 'I have some images of our house, and the school I went to. Children I played with. When I drove in from the airport I saw some trees that looked familiar. You'll probably think this sounds silly, but seeing them made me get all misty.'

'No. I don't think that's silly. I guess this must be quite an emotional time for you.'

Ariadne lowered her glance. 'You could say that.'

She felt surprised. There'd been sensitivity in his observation, almost like a friend. How ironic that, having dreaded meeting him almost to the point of nausea, as he was the only person she knew in the whole country she now dreaded the moment of saying goodbye to him.

That poignant song wafted from inside, winding its way in among her emotions. As she fielded Sebastian's questions about her life in Naxos the singer brought the melody to a crescendo of yearning that tore at her heart like a cry from across the sea.

*The silver moon, the evening tide*…how they evoked Naxos. She was swamped by a flood of homesickness, made worse by the knowledge she could never go back there now. Not now she'd sinned and they'd packed her off to the other side of the globe. Not now they'd hurt her.

Sebastian leaned beside her, caught a faint whiff of some enticing flowery perfume, and moved a safer distance away. Her blue eyes were dark and unreadable, with an occasional glitter that came from within. He realised with a slight shock that a vein of sadness ran beneath her volatile mood.

Desire was singing a siren song in his veins, but he kept a tight rein on it. Beauty mixed with emotion and moonlight could tempt a man to do and say things he'd regret. If he didn't maintain strict control he'd be dragging her against him and kissing her, tasting her sensuous mouth, caressing her soft curves…

'So what do you plan to do on your holiday?' he said.

'I might travel around. See some of the country.'

'Do you have any relatives here from your mother's side? Grandparents?'

She gave a shrug. 'My Australian grandma died a couple of years ago. There are a few cousins I've never met. Just a great-auntie Maeve who lives somewhere on the coast. Well, used to. My parents took me to stay with her once for a holiday when I was very small.' She wrinkled her brow. 'It might have been called Noza. Nootza. Something like that. Is that a place?'

He frowned. 'Could you be thinking of Noosa?'

Her brows lifted. 'Could be. That sounds right, doesn't it? Oh, it was heavenly there. I remember the beach, and Mummy and Daddy being really happy.' After a second she said lightly, 'Is it far from here?'

Something in her voice made him turn to examine her face. 'Noosa's up north. In Queensland. About a day's drive from here, perhaps a couple of hours by air. It's a fairly popular tourist resort.'

'Oh, good, good.' After a second she cast him a veiled glance. 'Do you think Queensland has art galleries?'

He lifted his brows. 'Bound to, of some sort. But if you want to visit art galleries there are plenty right here in Sydney.'

'Oh. Yeah.' She lowered her lashes. 'Of course. There would be.'

'Are you interested in art? Your father was an artist, wasn't he?'

She looked quickly at him. 'How do you know that?'

'My grandmother remembers who's who in everyone's family.'

'Oh.' Even in the soft light from the restaurant he saw her flush. 'You checked up on me. They know.' Her voice grew hoarse, as if she was stricken with the news. 'Your—your family *know*. About the—the deal you made with my uncle.'

Shocked by the raw emotion in her voice, for a moment he couldn't answer, words were snatched from him. Then he said, 'No, no, they— They don't know anything. And I haven't signed anything.'

'Oh, you haven't signed. Great.' She gripped the rail as if to steady herself. 'So tell me, then, what did he offer you? Honestly, please.'

'You.'

Her flush deepened, then she covered her face with her hands. The strangled words were almost a cry. 'In exchange for what?'

Her pained mortification wrenched something deep in his guts. With shame he recognised he'd never once properly considered the transaction from her point of view. He'd always assumed she was compliant. Even when she'd told him she didn't intend to marry him, he'd assumed it had been out of pique and anger.

How had the uncle presented the deal to her? It was clear now it hadn't been her initiative at all, and she knew nothing about the blackmail. He tried to remember what she'd told him in the lobby. A holiday to see if they suited each other, wasn't that what she'd said? Was that how it had been sold to her?

Never mind that the deal was all but sewn up a week before she'd left home. She deserved to know the truth, but how much truth about her uncle could she take?

He said carefully, 'Peri has offered a contract to my company—Celestrial. We design satellite systems for all sorts of uses, including marine navigation. Your uncle wants to upgrade his fleets' equipment.'

'I see.' She held herself rigidly. Shadows under her eyes gave them a bruised look, but she maintained a stiff dignity, trying so hard not to betray her distress he felt moved. 'So—so what will happen now the deal's off? Without a wedding? Will that matter to your company?'

Again he felt ashamed. Here she was struggling with her own situation, and she was worrying about his. He had no right to place any more anxiety on her head, he saw now.

He gave an easy shrug, easier than the grim reality warranted. 'We have other clients.'

'Oh.' She expelled a breath. 'Good. Well, that's a relief, anyway.'

'So…' He glanced searchingly at her. 'When you said you came out here for a holiday, you were telling the truth?'

She glanced at him and he saw with a further shock that the sudden glitter in her eyes was a wash of tears. She lowered her gaze as if she couldn't face him and turned sharply away. 'Yes, ' she said in a choked voice. 'That was it. A holiday.'

A few strands of her hair were ruffled by the breeze. The sight of her vulnerable neck in the moonlight caused something to twist in his chest. He took her shoulders and turned her gently back to face him. 'Ariadne, listen… There's no need to…'

A ray of light caught the sparkle of a tear on her lashes, and he felt a dismayed, incoherent wave of tenderness, but how was he, a man and a virtual stranger, to comfort her? Unable to frame the appropriate words, he bent to brush her mouth with his. It was only the briefest of touches, but the contact to his starved lips was sizzling dynamite.

She didn't pull away. She stood absolutely immobilised as though poised on a heartbeat, her sweet face still turned up in the kiss position, her lashes fluttering down in languid expectation. For an instant the planet held its breath.

God, it had been so long. Unable to resist such enticement, he kissed her properly.

He felt the shock ripple through her slender frame. Her mouth quivered under his, and he felt the leap of response ignite in her deliciously soft, fiery lips. He pulled her hard against him, his own lips ablaze, wild to feel her breasts in friction with his chest, greedy to have all of her at once with every part of him.

He urged her lips into parting, then slipped his tongue into the intoxicating seduction of her wine-sweet mouth. The scents and flavours of champagne, freshness, flowers and sweet, primitive woman rose and mingled in his senses, binding him in eternal, erotic enslavement. Stroking her mouth into arousal with his tongue was his own delicious torture.

He heard her make a small involuntary sound in the back of her throat, so evocative of passion the thrill of victory roared through him.

He deepened his demand on her mouth. And she responded, clinging to him and kissing him back with all the fire and fervour a man could dream of igniting in a woman.

All at once she leaned into him like a collapse, her soft curves so yielding and pliant it was another total seduction. He was swept with a purely masculine triumph as he recognised the slight loss of traction in her ability to stand upright. The more boneless and giving she felt in his arms, the harder and more focused was his lust to possess her.

With the strongest effort of will he fought to hold back his erection, but could anything be more irresistible than a desirable woman on the verge of surrender? Like a molten torrent the hot blood surged to harden him unbearably.

The wild notion stormed his fevered brain that he could take her, right there and then, up against the wall of the Park Hyatt.

But he wasn't altogether lost to reality. His desire filled him to bursting point but he restrained his yearning to grind his aching rod into the cleft between her thighs, though he was fast approaching the moment of barely being able to draw a line in his mind between imagining the rapturous pleasure and experiencing it.

He kept his lustful hands from plundering her ripe breasts, though his palms ached for their lushness.

He was a civilised man, and, though no one else was close by, they were in a public place. She must have become alive to that fact at the same time, because she suddenly stiffened in his arms, broke the kiss and shoved at his chest.

Regretfully he fell back, the feel of her warm, fragrant body lingering in his arms, in thrall to her fresh sweetness to the depths of his being.

She gazed at him, her eyes dark and stormy with that voluptuous, erotic knowledge women's eyes possessed when they'd just been thoroughly kissed. He could see her panting, her breasts heaving alluringly beneath the confining dress.

'Shall we go somewhere for coffee?' he managed to say, smooth as ever under pressure.

She stared at him for a second as comprehension clicked his meaning into place, then blue fire flashed from her eyes. 'We shall do no such *thing*. You listen to me, Sebastian Nikosto. That—*that* was a mistake. You shouldn't have done that.'

Her sultry mouth was even more swollen. It was so damnably seductive, it took his brain a moment to register her displeasure.

'You had no *right*,' she gasped. 'Just because my uncle offered me to you, doesn't mean *I* have. I'm not freely available to you. I'm not a—a—a goat or a donkey you can just—just *use* for your pleasure.'

'What?' He felt so rocked by the accusation his own voice sounded like a growl from the pit. 'That's not what I… Look, I *know* that, Ariadne. I wouldn't try to…I'm not the sort of guy who—who…' Anger, pride and masculine honour sprang bristling to his defence, but he damped down the bitter, blistering words that could have risen to his tongue.

With as much dignity as possible for a man in the grip of a hard-on, he said, his voice crackling with the effort, 'In case you didn't recognise it, what you just experienced was a kiss. A genuine kiss. The sort of kiss a man gives a woman he feels some sort of— *Admires*, for God's sake. And I'm pretty well certain you were appreciating it as much as I was. Sorry if you feel guilty about it.'

He waited to hear what she would say, but she'd turned her back on him and was smoothing herself down and tidying her hair, brushing down her dress with her hands as if she'd just been in the jaws of a wild foaming beast and needed to remove all traces of him.

He gave her an extra moment to lessen the charges, but nothing came of it. Sebastian Nikosto wouldn't wait for ever, however desirable the woman.

'Goodnight, then.' He clipped his punishingly polite words to give them maximum bite. 'Sleep well.'

He turned rigidly and walked back into the restaurant, a boiling chaos thundering through his veins of outrage, astonishment, guilt and bloody, bloody desire.

She swept up beside him in a flowery cloud of that perfume that would haunt him for the rest of his life, stalked to the table they'd shared, and snatched up her purse and wrap.

'And please don't insult me any further by attempting to pay for my dinner, Mr Nikosto.' Her sweet, low voice throbbed with emotion. 'I'll pay for my own. And it's not goodnight, it's *goodbye*.'

Sebastian drove to the Celestrial office, took the lift up to his floor and strode to his desk. Without a second's pause he typed the email he knew he should have sent a week since.

To: Pericles Giorgias

Dear Mr Giorgias,

At Celestrial we conduct our business contracts with honour and transparency. As CEO of this company, I reject utterly all hidden clauses, including 'gentlemen's agreements' that cannot stand up legally or morally to the light of public scrutiny.

Celestrial withdraws from all negotiations with Giorgias Shipping.

Consider our association at an end.

Sebastian Nikosto.


His cursor hovered over the send button while frustration and desperation boiled in his soul. Hell, but of course he couldn't send it. He slumped in his chair.

Now what? Work all night to eliminate the taste of her?

He got up and paced the office, striving to focus his mind on the challenges ahead of him the next day, anything to wipe out of his head the woman and her outrageous reaction to a simple kiss.

But it wasn't just the kiss, was it? his uncomfortable conscience nagged. It was the situation. It was his idiocy in suggesting coffee. Why had he done it? He cringed to think of how inept he'd been.

God, had he been so long without a woman he could no longer recognise one who'd been brought up in the traditions?

He cursed himself for a fool, blundering into that kiss with such blind abandon. How could he not have read the signs? He couldn't believe his error of judgement. She'd looked shocked, and revealed an utterly devastating lack of experience.

Where had she been for the last sixteen years? Had Peri Giorgias wrapped his niece in cotton wool and kept her in a tower?

He hadn't asked for her, but, whether he liked it or not, however furious and enraged and maddened he felt by the situation, she was here now, dammit. Proud, touchy and—

Soft. Fragrant. Yielding to any enchanted fool who took her in his arms.

*Vulnerable*, for God's sake.

Against his will, he'd been moved by her. And however unpredictable and explosive a package she was, he felt responsible for her. Not that she'd ever allow him to set foot near her again.

He winced with the acknowledgement that some of the accusations she'd hurled at him could have had some basis of truth. Would he have succumbed to temptation so rapidly if he hadn't at some stage thought of her as his for the taking?

He threw himself in his chair and flicked through his program files, stared for minutes unseeing at the screen, then gave up. A hundred laps of the pool were what he needed, followed by a long cold shower.

The situation looked irretrievable. Even if he wanted to risk taking the marriage option he'd wrecked his chances now. And admit it. He *wanted* to see her again. Wanted to talk to her, watch her eyes light up when she laughed, listen to her surprisingly husky voice.

Feel her softness. He closed his eyes while his senses swam in recollection.

If he could just think of some way to make things right with her.

# CHAPTER FIVE

IT WAS too hot in Sydney, even in an air-conditioned hotel suite of the finer quality. And there was no use blaming the champagne. A woman suffering sleep deprivation and jet lag should have expected to be able to sleep, not to toss and turn on her pillow or lapse into fitful dreams about Sebastian Nikosto. Disturbing dreams. Sensual and erotic dreams.

Although, if she was still wide awake could they honestly be called dreams? Fantasies, more like. Fantasies where he kissed her and touched her in the places she'd been so wildly conscious of during that kiss.

But as for that crack he'd made at the end about her feeling guilty…

Guilty? Her? Was *she* the one who'd instigated the kiss? Certainly she'd been polite, and co-operated in the spirit of the moment, but that was because she'd been well brought up, she had good manners and he'd taken her by surprise.

Every time she thought of the moment his lips had touched hers her insides swirled helplessly with a warm, languorous pleasure. The experience had felt nothing like kissing Demetri. She'd thought she'd been in heaven kissing Demetri, but now she realised she might as well have been pressing her mouth to the mirror.

She smoothed her fingers experimentally over her lips. She'd read about that fiery sensation in romance novels, of course, but never imagined it actually existed. She'd known sexy kisses, sure, but she'd never experienced those little tongues of flame dancing along her lips. Privately, she couldn't deny it had been pretty overwhelming.

She wondered if Sebastian had felt the same sensation. Perhaps he had, because what else had he meant about going somewhere for coffee if not to bed with her? He'd wanted to make love, just like that, and for a wild moment, for just a brief, fleeting, minuscule fraction of an instant, she was tempted.

But he didn't know that, did he? Or did he? How could he have known? She realised then that she'd known pretty definitely that he'd wanted her, so he probably did know.

Oh, it was all so humiliating. How could she allow herself to feel the slightest bit of attraction to a man someone else had chosen for her? A man who stood to make a profit?

His stunned face when she was accusing him of taking advantage of her rose up in her mind and she grew hotly impatient with herself. For goodness' *sake*, if only she could stop dwelling on it. What did it matter? She'd never see him again, anyway, and that was how she wanted it.

She kicked off the covers and turned on her side, willing herself to fall asleep. She'd just closed her eyes when a weird vibrating buzz by the side of the bed alerted her to the fact that the hotel phone was ringing on its night setting.

Thea Leni? A reprieve?

She scrabbled for the phone, knocking nearly everything off the nightstand in the process. 'Yes?'

There was a very small pause, then the deep masculine voice sank through her. 'It's Sebastian. *Don't...*'

Her entire being sprang to vibrant, pulse-drumming attention.

'...hang up, Ariadne,' he was saying. '*Listen*, please. I just want to—say something.'

She shouldn't listen. She should hang up and avoid talking

to him ever again. But she held her breath and the phone with a faintly moistening grip.

'What—what is there to say?'

He sighed. 'Oh, Ariadne.' That sigh rustled through her and disarmed her utterly, so evocative it was of rueful, manly remorse and bewilderment. 'What isn't there to say? I haven't woken you, have I?'

'No, no, I—I'm in bed.'

There was a sudden dramatic silence, then another sigh. This one had a totally different quality.

'Are you? In bed?' Even without seeing him she could feel his slow sexy smile break out. 'Me too. I haven't been able to sleep for thinking of…tonight and…what happened.' His voice had deepened, and become darker and more velvet if possible, as if by proxy stroking her all over in lieu of his lean, bronzed hands. 'I just needed to tell you that—I'm sincerely sorry I upset you. *All*—all the times I've upset you.'

'Oh.' She struggled with whether or not she should forgive him. Would it be weak of her? Wasn't he just trying to talk her round? But she wanted to. She brightened at the thought that without anyone else in Sydney, possibly the country, she didn't have a choice.

Not to make it too easy for him though, she said sternly, 'Well, you know, you can't just go around kissing people.'

'I know.'

He sounded so contrite, she felt soothed enough to go on. 'Trapping people into having dinner with you, then talking them into walking in the dark with you, and…'

'I know, I know. It probably looked like that. Can you just consider for a minute that I might—that I just—sincerely wanted to get to know you?'

She was silent. 'Well, there's no way you can get to *know* someone from one dinner. Not enough to—kiss them. We were *strangers*. We're still strangers.'

'Not altogether. Not now. Now that we've…'

'Kissed?' The word came out so huskily she had to clear her throat.

This time she could feel his smile radiating down the airwaves like a warm Saharan breeze. 'Well, I *was* going to say broken bread together, but, now that you mention it, a kiss does rather focus your attention on a person, doesn't it? I think it can tell you a lot.'

A hot flush washed through her, possibly making her glow in the dark. What could he tell about her? She hoped he didn't guess she'd been lying here, unable to think of anything else except that kiss. Whether she'd performed her part well enough. How much better it might have been if she had more practice. How she might *achieve* such practice.

'Maybe,' she conceded. 'All right, then.'

'And—look, I have to say I don't think of you as being a donkey, or a goat.'

Suspecting that he might secretly be laughing at the passionate things she'd said, she retorted quickly, 'You knew what I meant!'

'I did, yes. I think I can understand. I wanted to tell you that I feel the deepest respect for you.' He exhaled a long breath. 'Oh. This is a damnable way to meet someone, isn't it?'

Her ears rang in disbelief. She was silent, straining to wrench the inferences from the words. Did he mean…*meet* someone? As in…?

After a while she ventured, 'What—do you mean?'

Now *he* was hesitating. 'I think you are aware that I find you very attractive.'

Her heart thundered into a drum roll. Now was the time to hang up on him. Stop him from saying another seductive, undermining word. But she held on, drinking in every gap, every pause and nuance of what came next like a swan under the spell of a sorcerer.

'Desire is an amazing thing, isn't it?' he went on, his voice grave now. Warm and serious and sincere.

She lay in the darkness, her heart thundering, breathing so fast, with no defences against the beautiful deep masculine voice vibrating through her body, playing on her emotions, saying the things she'd always dreamed a gorgeous man would say to her.

'...So stunning, and exciting, the way it hits you like a train. Even when you might expect to feel the very opposite, you see someone across a room and at once your body knows, even before your mind does. Do you know what I mean?'

She was knocked sideways, her heart a racing turmoil, her brain in shocked, incoherent confusion. 'Oh, well, yes, I know I guess, Sebastian, but...but I mean... I can't *say*... Anyway, look. I have to...I have to get up early in the morning. So...'

'Oh. So you'd better get some sleep. Goodnight, then, Ariadne.'

'Goodnight.' She breathed the last word so softly it was hardly more than air, while her racing pulse roared in her ears.

Sebastian closed his phone and lay in the dark, wondering how far he'd retrieved the situation, smiling to himself about the shyness and shock in her husky voice, imagining her lying in bed in her pyjamas. No, not pyjamas.

A woman like Ariadne would wear pretty, virginal night-dresses. Fine cotton embroidered by little Swiss nuns with lace attached. What did they call that stuff? Broderie anglaise. He supposed it would be pretty enough, but say she belonged to him, he'd have wanted her to wear delicate silks and satins with thin little straps. Filmy things.

The vision that had nearly overwhelmed him when she'd told him she was in bed came flooding back to swamp him. Her hair spread around her on the pillow, her slim body covered in some-thing diaphanous. Sweet, pointed nipples through the gauzy fabric.

He dragged a pillow against him and groaned.

God, it had been too long.

* * *

Ariadne was up soon after dawn. After that call it had taken ages to fall asleep, but at least the jagged emotions of the disagreement had been smoothed away. Admit it, she'd been excited, going over every little thing Sebastian had said. At the time some of the things had moved her with their conviction, but now in the cold light of day she needed to try to be honest with herself.

What had really changed? Tempting as it might be to allow herself to be carried away, she mustn't forget that he had an incentive. Still, she wished she had at least said goodbye to him.

She was too worried about the bill to order breakfast, and besides, how could anyone eat with their life hanging in the balance?

When she was nearly ready to leave, she spread out the small collection of jewellery she'd thought appropriate to bring on a short holiday. Her earrings were all quite good, though she doubted she could get much for them, even if she found a jeweller who would accept them in exchange for cash.

She doubted her ruby pendant would buy her a bed for the night, let alone a plane ticket and a week or two's accommodation in Queensland. Then there was her watch. She laid it on the console table and tried to reconcile the idea of selling it with sentiment and guilt. It had been her mother's, one of the few reminders she had of that beloved face.

No, not that. Never. She couldn't bear to part with it.

The most valuable item was the sapphire bracelet Thio and Thea had given her when she'd turned twenty-one. The sapphires were finely matched Ceylonese, lavender-tinged blue and wrought with white gold. She adored the exquisite thing. The thought of selling it, when they'd loved her so much in the giving of it…

Her eyes started pricking again and she fought off the emotion and thrust those thoughts away. If they'd loved her, why had they done this terrible thing?

She fastened on the watch, and rolled the other items carefully back in their velvet pouches, slipping the earrings and the wrapped bracelet into her jacket pocket. She'd read of poor people selling their jewels to pawnbrokers, but Thea always dealt with Cartier. The bracelet had probably come from one of their boutiques, anyway. Surely they'd be happy to buy it back.

With her bags assembled ready for the porter, she located a phone directory, then reefed through it. There was a Cartier in Sydney, and hundreds of other jewellers, though she had no idea whether the addresses placed them near or far.

Perhaps the concierge could help.

Downstairs, she faced the reception clerk with a certain amount of trepidation. Her suite was opulent, even by the standards she'd been used to when she'd travelled with her aunt, so she could expect the cost to be high. Even so, when they handed her the account she was staggered.

She stared at it with disbelief, dismay clawing at her nape. Who'd have guessed champagne was so expensive? And why had she ordered so many courses without even checking to see what things cost? Guiltily, she realised she'd hardly even done justice to the meal, she'd been so churned up.

And why, for heaven's sake, had she needed an entire suite? Had Thio ever in his life been content to book a single room?

She stared at the invoice for a few moments, then looked the clerk in the eye and signed the credit-card slip as coolly as if she were rich and had the full backing of Giorgias Shipping.

Another night like this, though, and she'd be cleaned out. She'd have to think of something fast.

The concierge agreed to keep her suitcase safe until she returned. He obligingly scanned his computer screen for her when she enquired about jewellers, then produced a map of the city and ringed an address for her. Within walking distance, he said.

* * *

Sebastian made a deliberate effort to relax on his drive to work. In spite of a strenuous and bracing early-morning surf, the song that had haunted him through the night continued to echo in his mind. Ariadne, Ariadne...

How successful had he been in recovering ground with her? Perhaps she'd agree to meet him later. Maybe he could even take this weekend off to show her some of the sights. How long since he'd taken a weekend?

With an effort, he focused on the day ahead. Gloom had settled over the company, and it was becoming a difficult place to be. He knew his employees were asking questions about the Giorgias Shipping bid. Where was it heading? If there wasn't some sort of contract in the offing this week, any contract, he had some hard decisions ahead of him.

Trouble was, the place he really wanted to go right now was the Hyatt, to drown himself in blue eyes. This was hardly the way to deal with a crisis. The stress must have been getting to him.

Ariadne stalked numbly out of the pawnshop and into the street. She hadn't expected much cash for her earrings, but the amount the broker had offered for the sapphire bracelet had been pitiful. Surely they must be worth thousands. Thea never bought poor jewellery, not for a gift, not for anything.

If the salespeople at Cartier's hadn't been so suspicious and mistrustful when she'd offered to sell it to them, she'd have thought to have it valued so she'd at least know what sort of price to bargain for. As it was, she'd been lucky to escape from the shop without the police being called.

She broke out in perspiration as for a wild second she teetered on the verge of real panic. Conscious of an unpleasant sensation of nausea, she had to fight to steady herself enough to hang onto her control.

She leaned back against a shop window while she cooled down enough to think. There was no use sinking down onto the pavement. She could *earn* money, and when she had enough she'd buy her bracelet back from that sleazy pawnshop.

What she needed was to find a way to solve her situation. She forced herself to concentrate on her map, clinging to its solid reality like a lifeline. When her hot, scared pulse had subsided, she picked herself up and headed away from this dingy section of the city, back in the direction of the glossy shopping malls and department stores where she felt safer, enviously aware of all the happy-go-lucky Australians who took their homes and means and shelter for the night so cheerfully for granted.

Somehow, she would have to find work and a place to stay *quickly*. Surely accommodation would be cheaper outside the city?

The Centrepoint Arcade looked like a promising centre for internet cafés. She rode up and down escalators, tramped through the labyrinth of byways, until she found one and was able to log onto a computer.

Flights to Queensland weren't very expensive, she discovered, but accommodation in Noosa was. With a growing sense of dismay she scrolled through list after list of Noosa hotels. In Australia it was midsummer, the high season. There were a few vacancies left in cheaper places for backpackers, but she shrank from the idea of sharing accommodation with strangers. Did she even really want to go to Queensland now?

If she risked money to travel to Noosa and stay for the several nights, maybe weeks, it would take her to find a job, what guarantee did she have that Maeve still lived there? And how would she find her? She wasn't even sure of Maeve's surname. Her mother had been a Hughes, but a five-year-old would hardly have been aware of Maeve's family name.

And what would she do if she found her? Throw herself on Maeve's mercy? If Maeve had been the slightest bit interested in her existence, wouldn't she have contacted her after her parents died?

Without a secure money supply, the whole scheme started to look like a wildly impossible fantasy.

She spent a long time working out the intricacies of trawling through job registers, and saw with a sinking heart that it might not be as easy to find work in an art gallery as she'd hoped, even in a smaller centre. According to these websites, people needed as much documentation to prove their credentials and experience here as they did in Athens, and hers were all behind her in Naxos.

In desperation, she considered emailing Thea with an urgent request to send on her documents, then dismissed the idea. How likely was Thea to help her?

She slumped back in the chair. The naivety of her plans homed in on her. She knew one definite person in Australia, and here she was, rushing to get as far away from him as quickly as possible.

She needed help, but there was no way she could surrender to her uncle's plan by begging Sebastian for it. Her pride smarted fiercely at the thought of that. Unless she could think of some way to re-open negotiations without losing face…

One thing she'd learned during the Demetri crisis was that, whatever the fallout, she had to be true to herself. No matter how desperate she was, there was no way she would go on her knees to Sebastian in the role of victim.

And after that call last night, it was clear *what* he would think if she went to him. If he believed she was attracted to him…

Oh, please. Who did she think she was kidding? He believed it, all right. He knew it. Why else would he have said those things? He'd practically spelled it out.

If she went to him and told him she was without money, she'd have no bargaining power. What would he do—write her a cheque? She couldn't accept that. Anyway, he'd be much more likely to take her home with him. He'd be throwing her into his bed and having his way with her in no time, with no ring on her finger.

She'd be in an even worse position than a mail-order bride, reduced to being a casual fling, with no long-term security, her faith and upbringing betrayed, her conscience on fire for the rest of her life.

For the thousandth time the prospect of her own money sitting there in some solicitor's trust fund glowed in her mind with frustrating allure. If only she could get her hands on it. Even if it only amounted to a few thousand dollars, from where she stood now it would look like security.

She tried not to panic, but she knew she'd have to be quick. If she was in Sydney for long, last night had shown her how rapidly she'd eat up her little fund of money out of pure ignorance of the cost of ordinary things. Even when she'd been working in Athens, her flat and household expenses, including the domestic staff, had all been paid by her uncle.

She was green, that was her trouble. But no way was she a useless hothouse flower, as the tabloids had painted her, with no useful knowledge of the world except how to dress and how to look at a painting. Her aunt and uncle had seen her job as a nice little way to fill in time while she waited for her real purpose in life to be established, but she'd loved her career and taken it seriously. She'd run the acquisitions department at the gallery like clockwork until the scandal had caused her sacking. One rude assistant had described her as the fairy-floss tyrant.

Anyway, she could run a household and manage a staff of eleven, more if required. Thea had done her best to shape her as a potential wife, making certain she could cook, even if it wasn't very likely she would ever have to on a regular basis. And she was a fast learner. Some men found her attractive, even if Demetri didn't. Some even *admired* her.

Her uncle had often laughed at how she made every personal decision with her heart and not her head. She'd accepted his analysis with pride, preferring to be described as a passionate idealist than as some ruthless, calculating machine of a woman.

But it was clear that if she was to survive, this time she would have to dredge up her hard-headed negotiating skills.

Somehow, despite her attraction to Sebastian Nikosto, she would need to bargain with him as coolly and dispassionately as ever her uncle had.

She stared unseeing at the computer screen, then slumped forward with her face in her hands.

If only she understood more about men. How much had that midnight phone conversation meant? He might just have been trying to smooth things over after the restaurant. Sweet-talking her. But why? Did he still have hopes of the marriage?

Perhaps it really had been a genuine kiss, and he was sincere. How on earth was she to tell?

# CHAPTER SIX

FEELING like an executioner, Sebastian listened to the discussion around the conference table with half an ear, his brows drawn. Which of his team would he let go? Shiny, fresh-faced Matt, who was only just starting out, straight from university, so thrilled to have found employment in the industry of his choice? Or Jake, with a wife and three kids to provide for? School fees and a mortgage. Then there was Sarah, a creative talent who showed real promise.

Once lost to Celestrial, the chances of replacing his carefully chosen designers with equal talents in some post-crisis future were slim. And how would they survive in the meantime?

He'd just roused himself to rejoin the discussion when Jenny, his warm, efficient PA, slipped into the room and caught his eye.

'Not now.' He frowned with a slight shake of his head.

'But…' There was hesitation in her hazel eyes, then with an unprecedented disregard for his rebuff, she leaned close and murmured in his ear, 'Mr Nikosto, she says it's urgent.'

Deep in Sebastian's entrails a nerve jumped. '*Who* says?'

Though he knew. With a soaring anticipation in his chest, he knew.

Jenny lowered her voice even further. 'A Miss Giorgias. She says she's leaving Sydney in an hour, but she's prepared to give you some time to talk if you come at once.'

'Thanks.' He gave her a nod, then rose and excused himself. He strolled to his office, still cool and in control though an exultant expectation was rising in him like foam.

He reached for his desk phone. Steady, he warned himself. He put the phone to his ear, said without expression, 'Sebastian.'

He heard her small intake of breath, the slight hesitation, and his pulse quickened with the most thrilling suspense.

'It's—Ariadne.' There was commotion in the background that suggested a busy public place. 'If you would— If you would care to, I have a little time to talk to you before I leave.' Her voice sounded breathless, as if she'd been running. Or felt nervous.

He was plunged into a turmoil of conflicting desire and responsibility. 'I'm involved here today. I can't—'

'Oh, well, it doesn't matter,' she said at once. 'I don't really have time either. I guess I'll just say—'

'Where are you?'

'I think it's…er…Pitt Street and Market. In a phone booth, near a café called The Coffee Club.'

For a wild, wavering instant he tossed up his competing urgencies. Glancing at the desk clock, he saw it was nearly morning teatime. Supposing he sprinted all the way…

He issued a command. 'Stay there. Don't move.'

He punched in a call to Jenny, gave her some brisk instructions, then took the lift down to the ground floor. As soon as he was on the street he broke into a run. With the adrenaline singing in his veins he hardly noticed the shoppers as he cut through the crowds like a home-running champion whizzing through the bases. He grinned at furious drivers pumping their horns when he dodged them at the crossings, and flew the five city blocks in a matter of minutes.

Once in the Pitt Street Mall, though, he paused to catch his breath, smoothed his hand over his hair, checked his tie was in place, shirt tucked in. Then, energised, his capillaries tingling to the scent of victory, he headed for the Market Street end.

The café was easy enough to locate. He zeroed in on her standing to one side of the entrance, her bag slung casually from her shoulder. At first sight of her desire quickened his blood like an aphrodisiac.

Her blonde hair rippled down her back and she was wearing sunglasses, slim, sand-coloured trousers that hung from her hips and a pretty white short-sleeved top. Simple, classy and sexy. Oh, so sexy.

He started forward, then restrained himself to a casual stroll.

Ariadne scanned the crowd, her nervous pulse bumping along. She was about to take the most enormous risk. The possibilities of humiliation were so extreme she felt almost faint. She was gambling on making her offer sound businesslike, a simple contract. If only she could manage to control her responses to him and stay cool and clear-headed.

'Hi.'

She started as Sebastian's deep voice cut through her anxious churnings and swivelled around. His handsome face was smooth and expressionless, his dark eyes veiled.

'Oh, hi,' she breathed, overwhelmed by the immediacy of his lean, dark sexiness in the raw, masculine flesh. She felt burningly conscious of those words that had thrilled down her spine during the midnight call. 'You—you didn't take long.'

His searching gaze swept over her, not missing a thing. She prayed she didn't look desperate, or too rounded in the hips and bust as Demetri had once criticised. Then his eyes lit with a smile, and she remembered what he'd said about desire hitting you like a train.

'It's not far.' He shrugged. 'People are waiting for me, so I can't give you much time.' He glanced at his watch, then indicated the café entrance. 'Do you want to go inside?' He made to take her elbow, but his hand just stopped short of touching her.

She walked into the café ahead of him, sensing his gaze scorching down her spinal column while she racked her brains for a way to begin. He was in a different mode from the man who'd talked so sweetly to her in the night. He looked serious and inaccessible, a CEO with his mind on his work.

He pointed her to a vacant table and she sat down, trembling all at once with the risk of the gamble she was about to take.

'So?' His acute gaze penetrated through to the back of her brain as if he could read all the lies she'd ever told, all her fears and failings, her empty bank account, the Demetri scandal, her uncle and aunt and their low trick.

Ariadne drew in a long breath and met his gaze. 'All right. I've made a decision. I'll do it.'

His eyes sharpened. 'Do what?'

It took her a moment to frame the words. 'Marry you.' She clenched her hands in her lap.

He stilled. The lines of his face grew focused and intent. Her words seemed to crash in the air around them. It was as if the entire café receded into the distance, and he and she were the only people in the world. She had a dim realisation of the enormity of her offer.

He sat studying her face with a frown. 'Let me get this straight. You're now asking me to marry you. What makes you think I want to get married?'

*Thunk*, went her heart, then started knocking against her ribs.

He lowered his black lashes, then gave a quizzical shrug. 'I'm not sure I know what to say.'

She felt heat flood her. The ground under her suddenly shifted. With a terrible embarrassment she realised she'd assumed too much, thinking he'd ever been willing. Aware of her cheeks burning, she tried to think of an excuse for her ghastly blunder. 'I thought you said—my uncle had offered your company a contract.'

'I didn't say I'd accepted it.'

He was playing it cool but alluring images were flashing through Sebastian's mind. The contract with Giorgias Shipping, signed and sealed. Celestrial on solid ground, his workforce safe and secure. He thought of the faces around the conference table that morning, the unspoken anxiety that hung over the office. How it would feel to tell them all the company's worries were over.

He contemplated the woman seated across the table from him and felt a dangerous excitement streak through him. Her blue eyes were cool and guarded, her delicious lips slightly parted, as if she was holding her breath. So kissable. He remembered the taste of her, the fragrance of her skin and hair.

Warning bells clanged Esther in some cautious part of him, perhaps he should pull back, but her sweet femininity drew the beast in him like honey. He tried not to dwell on her mouth, her satin throat, the smooth skin disturbed by one tiny, nervous pulse as she waited in taut anticipation of his response.

He mustn't let desire rule him. He'd vowed never to marry again, remember? He refused to be blackmailed. Still…

She was so mouth-wateringly desirable. And last night had demonstrated pretty clearly how far he was likely to get with her if it wasn't legal.

Ariadne held her breath, trying to read his face, intensely aware of his scrutiny.

He said softly, 'Do you propose to every man who tells you he desires you?'

His directness rocked her again, just as it had in the night. She felt intensely aware of his lean, supple hands relaxed on the table, the dark shadow outlining his chiselled mouth. But she needed to keep her head.

She gave a shrug, just as if her pulse wasn't racing. 'Only if they've just been offered a big fat juicy contract to take me on.'

He broke into a laugh, but there was ruefulness in its tone. 'Poor Ariadne.'

She clung to her cool façade. 'This is just a wedding I'm talking about. A business contract, pure and simple. No—'

The corners of his mouth edged up and he said, his voice softly mocking, 'No what? Passion?'

She felt a deep internal lurch. 'Oh. Oh, well…'

His mouth was grave, but his eyes were suddenly heavy with sensuality. She broke off, realising he was loving this, teasing her, saying sexy things he knew affected her, keeping her in suspense.

His gaze flickered over her and she felt singed. 'What happened to only marrying people on equal terms? Or did I dream that?'

'No, you didn't dream it. But you aren't the only one who has something to gain from the marriage. I—I do too.'

'What?' He examined her face, his dark eyes shimmering. 'Now you're sparking my imagination. What could possibly make it worth your while to become my wife?'

She risked meeting that scorching-hot gaze again. 'When I get married, I can claim my inheritance. From my parents. Otherwise I have to wait until I'm twenty-five.' The smile in his eyes was doused, and she added quickly, 'We'd only have to stay together a few days. After that, you can go your way and I'll go mine. You see? Everyone wins.'

She glanced up as a waitress approached with a notebook and pencil. Toast and hot chocolate, a flat white. 'Do you have orange juice?' she enquired.

Sebastian marshalled his critical faculties and considered the facts, such as they'd been presented.

Remembering her distress last evening, he was surprised. Why had she suddenly come around to the marriage she so despised? He doubted now it had much to do with his lust-driven midnight call. Could money be an issue with her? But how was that possible? Could she have fallen out with her uncle and aunt?

He drummed his fingers on the table, trying to reconcile his conflicting instincts, only too blazingly conscious of her blue eyes, the sweet lips that had haunted his sleep.

She had her hair tucked back behind ears as delicately curved as cockleshells. Her slim neck held her graceful head upright, like the stem of a flower, a proud, soft, heartbreakingly beautiful flower.

To have her for a few days, or not to have her at all?

Marriage sounded so final, but this one wouldn't be genuine. There'd be no emotional demands, no risk of loss here. No horror or heartache to weigh him down for years to come. A few days would pass like a flash.

What did the man who'd already lost everything have to lose?

Anyway, he hardly ever spent time at home. How badly could it disturb his comfort to have a woman waiting in that empty, soulless house for him for a few evenings?

A woman whose luscious mouth had opened to him like a flower?

The food came, and he watched her wrinkle her nose as she tasted the orange juice.

She sipped her chocolate next, then spread butter over her toast. With graceful manners she offered him a piece, and when he refused he watched her bite into hers with her pretty white teeth. He sipped his coffee, gave her a moment to assuage her hunger, only just suppressing a groan.

Would a few days suffice to assuage his? A few nights? A thousand and one nights?

'Don't they do breakfast at the Hyatt?' Desire deepened his voice almost to a growl.

'They do, but I—didn't have time.' Finished her toast, Ariadne wiped her hands on her paper napkin, then glanced up to be trapped in his smouldering dark gaze.

'So you aren't prepared to marry a man who wants you for your money, but *you* are prepared to marry for money.'

'For my *own* money.'

His mocking words gave Ariadne the dismayed sense that she'd failed. He might be burning her to the floor with his eyes, but that didn't mean he was prepared to marry her. He was just toying with her. So what now? Beg him to give her a bed for the night? But it would be his bed, wouldn't it?

Desperation had brought her to this, and pride was all she had now to fall back on. Time to get out before she made an even bigger fool of herself.

She found a note in her purse, laid it down beside her cup, then stood up. 'All right, forget I mentioned it. It was a mistake. I thought you wanted a—a deal. I must have—misunderstood.'

She was on the way to sweeping out when his hand snaked out and gripped her wrist. For an instant she saw something else in his eyes. Amusement. Kindness.

'Hang on. Sit down a minute longer and tell me more. Just how do you envisage this deal working?'

Her crushed hope quivered, then sprang back to buoyant life. She hesitated, conscious of the burn of his fingers on her skin, then allowed herself to sit down again.

He waited, his mouth grave, and so stirringly sexy she couldn't help thinking of how it had felt when he'd pressed his lips to hers. That fiery sensation still seemed to linger in her nerve fibres.

She drew a breath. 'Well, first I considered getting a marriage certificate somehow and faking it…'

He held up a hand, shaking his head. 'Stop right there. This is Australia. You can be done for fraud here as fast as blinking. For God's sake, never try to mess with a legal process that involves money *here*.'

She nodded. 'That's why I decided I might as well go through with the real thing. I don't want anything else from you. All I need is to marry you today.'

He blinked. 'Today?'

'Yes. Then I'll fax the marriage certificate to my uncle, he can notify the lawyers and have my inheritance transferred into my bank account, and I can get on with my life. And you can get on with yours.'

'Whoa, hold on.' The separate pieces of information lodged themselves into Sebastian's brain, but, focusing on the most immediate, he held up a hand. '*Today*. I don't think so. I told you, there are laws in this country.'

'No,' she said, her face as earnest and innocent as a nun's. A sexy, determined nun. A nun whose smooth breasts were screened by little more than a couple of thin layers of cotton fabric. 'I looked it up just now on the Internet. You can get the court officials to grant you a licence if you have a good reason.'

'Right.' He shook his head disbelievingly, although he had an inkling that what she'd said might be true. She'd done her homework well. It was clear Miss Ariadne Giorgias really wanted to marry him. Today. For whatever reason.

Even in thrall to lust, he had to wonder what the emergency was.

'Ah,' he said, his voice deepening, 'just supposing for a crazy moment I were to consider it, I'm not sure what that good reason would be. So I can assist a rich woman to get richer?'

'I'm not rich,' she said quickly. 'If you expect that you'll be disappointed. I just want what belongs to me.' Then she lowered her lashes and added quietly, 'Anyway, if you don't care to, it doesn't matter. I'll probably go back to Greece.'

Intrigued, he realised that for some reason, she needed to get married fast. And whether she knew it or not, her threat had genuine potency. He didn't want her to go back to Greece. Not yet.

His gaze drifted to her shoulders and arms. The feel of her ached in his memory. He itched to take her arms in his hands, feel their soft, toned resilience. Instead, he reached across and took her hands.

'So tell me. What's the big rush?'

Her slim hands trembled in his grasp, and her gaze flooded with an awareness that sent the hot blood coursing to his loins. Nothing could have been more seductive than to inspire that look in a beautiful woman.

But almost at once she pulled away and tucked her hands out of reach, her gaze guarded. No touching, he understood. Not until it was legal.

'Well, it's—it's just a matter of timing.' She evaded his eyes. 'I'm not planning to stay in Sydney long, so it makes sense to do it at once. The sooner I marry, the sooner I'll have my inheritance. Why wait?'

'What about your dress, the church, the photographer? They all take time. And don't you want to give your aunt and uncle plenty of notice? Surely you want them at your wedding?'

'*No*.' Her hands flew up in agitation. 'Absolutely *n*—' She pulled herself up and said in a low, firm voice, 'I—I don't want to bother them with it. I don't want to bother anyone.'

'I see.' He considered her a moment. 'As it happens, I have a grandmother, parents, two sisters and a brother who'd almost certainly feel cheated if I didn't invite them to my wedding.'

'Please.' Her blue eyes widened in horror. 'I can't do it at all if I have to have a big ceremony and all that publicity. I'd really much prefer it if we kept it a secret from people here.'

He raised his brows, then remembered her distress last night at the thought of the uncle's deal being known. Still, he couldn't imagine keeping a bride concealed for long from his highly inquisitive family. 'Are you sure you know what you're doing? Families have a way of finding things out.'

Her face tensed. 'Oh. Do you live with yours?'

'Hell, no, thank God. They live across the bridge, and I live at Bronte Beach.' He was touched with a slight discomfort then about what they would think if they knew any of this. Him taking up with a woman so spontaneously, after Esther and all she'd suffered. At least, that was how it would appear.

'Why? Don't you like them?' Her anxious blue glance drew him.

'I *like* them. It's just that I have to keep a distance from them or they'd kill me with kindness.'

Her shoulders relaxed and she brightened. 'Good. Then what's the worry? And anyway, how could you even *think* of wanting it in a church with the priest and the holy sacraments? We'll be divorcing just as soon as we can. It'd be a—*sacrilege.*' She gazed at him with scandalised reproach, then shook her head and sighed. 'Don't they have places here for things like this where you can just have a civil wedding? Without all the stuff? Just someone to say the words, then you sign something?'

He made a wry grimace. 'Sure. They have that. I thought it was the life goal of most women to have all the stuff.'

She looked quickly at him, and he realised he'd struck some sort of chord. She said emphatically, 'Not me.' Then she leaned forward, her eyes suddenly blazing, her cool thrown to the winds. 'Look, if you don't want to do it, it's all right, I don't either, not really. It was a stupid idea. Let's forget the whole thing.'

Sebastian heard himself say coolly, 'Relax. I'll do it.'

'Oh,' she breathed, sitting back. 'You will?' The relief sparkling from her blue eyes sent his curiosity skyrocketing. What was going on? 'Today?'

He shrugged. 'If I can organise the licence. There's no guarantee, mind, but I'll get my lawyer to give it a shot. You'd better give me your passport. There's bound to be miles of red tape.'

She handed him a slim zip-purse with her passport and travel documents. He slipped it in his pocket, then took her hand across the table and held it. The hand was warm and trembling, her shy, glowing eyes the same cerulean blue as the sky.

He felt a giddy burst of desire-driven euphoria. 'You won't regret it.'

'Of course not.' She gave him an unsure smile. 'We both have something to gain.'

But he could feel her palm zinging against his like a butterfly wing. His heart accelerated to a strong certainty that his instincts about her were correct. She wanted him, he felt sure of it. He could feel the leap of response in her every touch and glance. Despite her cool little negotiation, there was passion in her, and tonight it would be his to unlock.

A shadow hovered at the edge of his mind but he pushed it back and rose to his feet, glancing at his watch. Just about time to get back for his next meeting. Though God knew how he'd concentrate for the rest of the day on such mundane things as satellite systems when he had a wedding ahead of him. A wedding *night*.

He whipped out a card and wrote his number on the back. 'Here. I'll phone you at the hotel when I've arranged things.'

She hesitated, then said lightly, 'It might be better if I phone you.'

'Fine.' He touched her cheek, and made a gruff attempt to soothe away the aftermath of last night's angry exchange at the restaurant. 'I'm—glad you feel better today.'

Her lashes lowered. 'Well,' she murmured. 'At least we know where we stand now.'

Do we? he wondered on his athletic dash back to Celestrial. Where did *he* stand? Or was he floating on high above the moon? Wherever, it felt like a very unstable, rocky location, for a man used to navigating space without fear. But he was getting married in just a few short hours. Exciting, the night ahead. Crazy, perhaps even dangerous, but it was a long time since he'd felt so exhilarated.

So—*alive*.

# CHAPTER SEVEN

THE lobby at the Park Hyatt was so busy with the midweek arrivals and departures of guests, that in all the bustle no one seemed to notice when Ariadne dropped off to sleep behind her magazine. Eventually something woke her, and her immediate panicked thought was that she'd forgotten to phone Sebastian. She calmed down when she realised it was only three, and made for the public phone.

The licence had been arranged, Sebastian informed her, and his PA had been working on the wedding all day long. A celebrant had been located, and Sebastian would pick her up just before five. Ariadne galvanised herself to action, retrieving her suitcase from the concierge and taking it to the Ladies' to search for a more appropriate wedding outfit.

The amazing success of her gamble at the café had left her feeling exhilarated at first, then caution had crept in. Her financial problems were all about to be solved, but the possibilities of what might happen after the wedding began to consume her. Sebastian was no preening butterfly, vacillating between mistresses. If he wanted a woman, she felt sure he'd be direct about it. She thought of his straight dark gaze, and a flame curled her insides.

He desired her all right, she realised with an accelerating heartbeat. Would he expect her to sleep with him when it was merely a marriage of convenience? Without the blessing of the church?

She should have talked about it to him at the café. She wished she'd had the poise to bring it up at once and deal with it gracefully. Somehow, she'd have to try to settle it before the ceremony.

How easy would it be to talk to him about the delicate subject? Last night on the phone he'd had no trouble talking about his attraction to her, but she doubted she'd ever be able to say things like that.

She'd always dreamed her husband would be someone she knew very well, someone who understood her and loved her, even so. With a grimace she realised that so far neither of her potential bridegrooms had fitted the profile.

She chose one of the little suits she'd had made in the Rue du Fauborg St Honoré for her intended honeymoon with Demetri. It was cream with the palest of pink and blue threads running through it, and thin edgings of cream lace at the cuffs and lapels. It cinched in at the waist and buttoned at her breast, with a hint of cleavage just visible. She'd never worn it, so it wasn't as tainted as some of the clothes she'd discarded from her trousseau.

This wasn't a wedding in the true sense but, even so, she wanted to look pretty. She wound her hair into a loose bun and threaded a blue ribbon through it.

When Sebastian arrived, for the first few moments she felt quite overwhelmed. He'd gone to so much trouble, she was momentarily speechless. He looked so handsome and austere in a beautifully tailored black three-piece suit, elegant white shirt and white silk tie with a silver stripe, like a genuine bridegroom. Somehow, though, the fine clothes only made her more aware of the raw animal man confined inside.

He swept her with a hot shimmering gaze that sent a wild surge through her veins.

When she'd collected herself, she said, 'You look *gor*— Very wedding-i-fied.'

Amusement gleamed in his eyes, but there was a searing sensual intensity in them that told her clearly what was uppermost in his mind. When he spoke his voice deepened.

'Likewise.'

Her nerves jumped. Maybe it was her imagination, but the air seemed rife with sexual vibrations. He bent to kiss her, and his sexy lips missed her mouth and just brushed her cheek. Even so her senses spun into dizzy overload.

He took her bags and piled them into the boot of his car, then held the door for her. 'Ready?'

As they swept out of the drive of the Park Hyatt into the maze of city streets she felt a moment of deep insecurity. She hardly knew him. What had she let herself in for?

After only a few twists and turns through the heavy traffic— hair-raising to someone used to driving on the other side of the road—he swerved into the kerb and parked. He hustled her out of the car and onto the street, and she was faced with the façade of the jewellery boutique she'd braved that morning.

She gulped. 'Oh. Are we going in there?'

'We need to pick up our rings. Come on,' he said, shepherding her relentlessly through the doors. 'They're expecting us.'

She reminded herself she was wearing different clothes. Perhaps they wouldn't recognise her. Once inside the glossy interior, she glanced about at the sales people, then tried to nudge Sebastian in the direction of one she hadn't dealt with in her morning visit.

The attempt was useless, because the manager of the boutique caught sight of them and came out of his office, rubbing his hands. He greeted Sebastian warmly, and looked keenly at her as if she reminded him of someone. To her intense relief, he mentioned nothing about their previous encounter.

Several trays of rings were placed before them. Sebastian was more careful and discerning than she'd expected, considering they were in a hurry. She was so anxious to escape from the shop she'd have agreed to anything, but they managed at last to find beautiful, plain bands in matching rose gold, Sebastian's heavy and solid, hers finer and more delicate.

The manager suggested they have them inscribed, and surprisingly Sebastian was keen to go to the trouble. There was a small discussion, and in the end it was decided to have their initials entwined, along with the date and the word 'Eternity'. She prickled with impatience, desperate not to wait the few extra minutes it would take.

'What about your engagement ring, though?' Sebastian said, advancing on a display case bright with diamonds. 'You should have one of these.'

'Is that really necessary?' she exclaimed.

He gave her a firm look. 'Absolutely, though on second thoughts... No, I think a sapphire. What do you think?' He smiled, the glow of desire in his gaze. 'Could there be a sapphire to match those eyes?' Before she could reply he turned to a hovering sales assistant. 'Sapphires. Do you mind?'

It was the same man she'd dealt with in the morning.

'By all means,' he said with an oily smile. He unlocked a cabinet and laid a tray of blue brilliants before them on the counter. 'Felicitations, Miss Giorgias. Oh, and...er...did you manage to find a satisfactory broker for your bracelet?'

Sebastian's surprised gaze swivelled around to examine her face, and she felt herself blush to the roots of her hair. 'No, no...well, yes...sort of, thank you,' she mumbled.

'Very fine stones,' the assistant murmured. 'Very fine indeed. Sorry we couldn't...er...accommodate you.'

The bland apology came too late, and at the worst possible time. She participated in the selection of an exquisite sapphire ring set in diamonds with her brain only half engaged. The other half was busy worrying about Sebastian having been alerted to her desperate situation.

She escaped from the shop, shards of blue fire flashing from her finger. It was a fine stone, and had cost no mean price for a temporary arrangement. She felt guilty at causing Sebastian such expense, and hoped he could afford it. But at least now he would be able to benefit from her uncle's deal.

He returned to the car and tossed the package into her lap. He turned to scan her face with his acute dark gaze, but didn't question her about the sapphires. She might have been imagining it, but he seemed extra silent and thoughtful for the rest of the journey.

After that everything took place at high speed. It was only a brief journey to the home of the wedding celebrant, where Sebastian's lawyer, Tony, and a woman from his office he introduced as Jenny, were waiting in a small courtyard at the front.

'Witnesses,' Sebastian explained.

The men shook hands, and Tony and Jenny kissed Ariadne, just as if she were a real bride. It was just a marriage of convenience, she kept reminding herself. She had made that clear, hadn't she?

They were about to ring the doorbell when Sebastian made a small exclamation and hurried back to the car. He returned with a bouquet of pink and white roses, fragrant with white stars of jasmine and orange blossom.

'Here,' he said. 'Hold this.'

While Ariadne clutched it, he nipped off a rosebud and tried to thread it through his buttonhole, his sculpted, masculine lips pursed in concentration. Everyone watched while he struggled. Eventually he stuck it in place at a slightly crazy angle. No one else offered to fix it, and in the end Ariadne was forced to give the bouquet to Jenny and fix it herself.

She stepped close to him, searingly conscious of the thinness of the layers of clothes between her breasts and his bare chest, the seductive shadow on his smooth-shaven jaw. As she performed the intimate little task before the interested onlookers, she felt his sensual gaze on her face, and knew she was going pink.

'There,' she said, risking meeting his eyes for a soul-scorching instant. He might have kissed her then, but he didn't. He was thinking of it though, she knew with a sudden certainty. Thinking of that, and the time after the ceremony when she would be his legal wife.

The celebrant, a middle-aged woman with a pleasant face, greeted them and ushered them all through the house to the garden in the rear.

The small party stood on a smooth velvet lawn in the rays of the setting sun. The hill sloped down to the sea, but Ariadne hardly registered the beauty of the surroundings. The entire event had taken on a surreal quality.

Sebastian was quiet, his face grave, but every time their eyes met his held a dark, possessive gleam that reached into her in some deeply stirring, primeval way she'd never experienced before with a man.

She was in such a haze she was hardly aware of the words of the ceremony. 'I, Ariadne Sarah Christiana...' she said at one stage. Then there was the moment when Sebastian slid the ring on her finger and promised to love and honour her. The look in his eyes was so intent, so serious, she felt a thrilled clench in her chest.

The celebrant pronounced them man and wife. There was a pause, while all held their breaths. Or it might have been that she was holding hers. Then Sebastian tilted up her face and kissed her. It was a gentle brushing of lips to begin with, then he subtly deepened the pressure. Her senses swayed as she felt him move a hand to her ribs and another to the small of her back.

A slow, sly flame licked through her lower abdomen. Her knees turned to water, and she melted into him, just as she had the night before.

In the nick of time Sebastian broke the kiss before it grew too intense to draw away from. Even so, that licking flame had infected her blood and she was left breathless, and just the slightest bit intoxicated. She became aware then of cameras flashing, someone throwing rice and confetti, and the dark triumphant gleam in Sebastian's eyes before his lashes flickered down to screen his gaze.

The wedding feast was in a private room at a restaurant, where toasts were drunk and course after course was placed before her, including a glistening slice of chocolate cherry torte. Tony and Jenny, strangers a few short hours since, were friendly and open and funny, and warmer to her by the minute, though she sensed the slight distance between Jenny and Sebastian that went with boss-employee relationships. Jenny was quite wary of him, Ariadne realised. Perhaps he was an exacting boss.

There was no dancing, no joyous bouzouki and loving celebratory family, but a chance to laugh with some new-found friends soothed her wounded heart and gave her worries some much-needed relief.

Added to that, seething somewhere inside her was a deep vein of excitement, a fever that grew in her blood every time her eyes fell on Sebastian's hands, or the lean, sinewy wrists bound by his elegant cuffs. Eventually the laughter and conversation reached a point when he said, 'Come, my sweet. I think it's time we left, and allowed Tony and Jenny to get on with their evenings.'

*My sweet.* That was what men called their wives. Their lovers. His gaze captured hers across the candle flame. He was smiling, his midnight satin eyes aglow with a dark sensual fire.

# CHAPTER EIGHT

ARIADNE stood before the front door of a cliff-side villa with a giant telescope on its roof, while her husband slid a key into the lock. Her legal husband.

During the feast, carried along by the atmosphere, she'd looked forward to being alone with Sebastian, but, now she was, misgivings had set in. How married were they? And how much of a wife would he expect her to be? The situation was so tenuous. Once she had her inheritance she would be on her way.

On the other hand, there had been something quite definite about that ceremony they'd been through. From his point of view, she supposed he'd carried out his side of the bargain. Her turn now, some inner voice prodded.

He opened the door and looked down at her with that fire in his eyes. 'Welcome home,' he murmured, slipping his arm around her waist.

Even smiling, his mouth looked so firm and capable. Capable of delivering ecstasy, she thought with a plunge in her insides.

His possessive hand on her ribs actually felt pleasant. He was in such a buoyant mood she wondered if she should remind him their marriage was only temporary.

'Thanks.' She drew in a breath. 'Do you...do you have a fax machine?'

His brows shot up, then came down again rather hard. 'Can't you worry about that tomorrow?'

'No,' she said firmly. 'Right now's the best time. Thio will be reading his messages now.'

'To hell with Thio,' he said forcefully. 'This is our wedding night.'

Without any warning he lifted her off her feet and into his arms, laughing at her shocked cry. Pressed against the wall of his chest, her sensitive flesh fairly tingled with electrical impulses. Even the sensation of his jaw grazing her forehead was distinctly pleasurable.

He carried her inside, pausing at some point to touch a switch with his elbow. Lamps came on in all directions.

As he strode with her through the house she got a confused impression of large airy rooms with high ceilings and wide windows, which revealed glimpses of the cliffs undulating around the shoreline, peppered with twinkling lights. He swept her up a flight of stairs, down a wide hall and through double doors into a huge bedroom, and halted there, holding her in his arms a second longer, his eyes agleam with triumph. His glance flicked to the bed, and for a nerve-racked second she thought he was going to toss her into the middle of it. She braced in readiness, then he checked the impulse, lightly kissing her lips before planting her on her feet on the rug instead.

'Just relax,' he commanded, his deep voice rich with satisfaction. 'I'll be back.'

Relax! She gazed around the alien space, intimate with another person's occupation. A male person's. The room had an extremely masculine feel, with solid, hard-edged furniture. On either side of some French doors, windows reached to the floor, with soft filmy white curtains adrift on the breeze while heavier dark red satin ones were bunched back. But what dominated the room was a large bed, luxuriously attired in rich dark red fabrics.

It had big snowy pillows, heaped to look inviting. And it was inviting. Its insidious message would have enticed even the wariest virgin to dive in, roll on its plush covers and wallow in its springy embrace.

Maybe it was just her, but that bed seemed to glow and vibrate and command attention. She noticed a black satin dressing robe draped over the end, and the large masculine slippers neatly aligned on the floor beside it. Someone had placed them there with care.

Sebastian returned with her suitcase and set it down inside one of several doors leading off from the bedroom. She followed him and saw it was an unoccupied dressing room with long glass mirrors. Adjacent to it was a rather sumptuous bathroom, also unoccupied.

'Oh. Is there—another bedroom through here?'

He undid his silvery tie, his eyes shimmering, then slipped it off and dropped it on the floor.

'Several, but ours is the only one fit for occupation.' A lazy, amused smile played on his mouth. 'No need to worry.' His voice grew husky as he took her wrists and ran his hands up her arms, sending thrills through her nerve endings. 'I think you'll find everything in *this* room more than adequate for your needs.'

Her skin cells seemed to have developed a will of their own. They were loving his touch through the jacket sleeves, were tuned into it one hundred per cent. Unfortunately, she needed to get some things clear in her head before things zoomed out of control.

He lifted his lean hands to cradle her face, but before he could press his lips to hers she seized his wrists to still them, and slipped from his grasp.

'I think we need to sit down and have a good chat,' she said, her voice rather higher-pitched than usual.

Sebastian narrowed his eyes and examined his bride. Though deliciously flushed from the champagne and the excitement, while she was clearly attempting to preserve her poise, her eyes were conveying a dark uncertainty.

He felt a pang of misgiving. Last night's choking moments after the kiss were etched into his soul, moments he would prefer never to revisit. The charge that he'd taken advantage of her had cut deep. For God's sake, he was hardly a wild animal. He was aware that a civilised man didn't ravish a tender woman at the first opportunity. And if she was as inexperienced as he suspected, it was only natural she'd be feeling a few nerves. Still, it was their wedding night, and anxiety should never be unnecessarily prolonged.

'Of course,' he said politely, bracing for the challenge. He stood back a little to give her some space. 'Are you—nervous about anything?'

Her chin came up. 'Nervous? I should say not. I just—just need to be clear about things.'

Ariadne saw determination settle into the lines of his chiselled mouth, and she was reminded of last night when she'd refused to have dinner with him. During the day she'd been so worried about her precarious situation, then so relieved to think she'd solved it, she hadn't had enough time to crystallise a plan.

Everything had happened so fast. But now that the moment had arrived, whatever her primal instincts had earlier been whispering, she had a conscience. A celebrant wasn't a priest. A garden wasn't a church. And despite the certificate Sebastian had slipped into the inner pocket of his jacket, their reasons for being married had very shaky foundations.

Looked at in the cold light of objectivity, a financial contract between virtual strangers was hardly an excuse for making love. Although, did she really need to look at the situation in the cold light of objectivity?

As she met Sebastian's speculative gaze, even thinking the words *making love* cast her insides into a swirling hot chaos. She wasn't exactly tipsy, but she wished she hadn't joined in quite so many of the toasts and could weigh the moral issues with more clarity.

Before he decided to pounce, she backed from the room, then turned and found her way rather quickly down the stairs and into a large sitting room.

Despite her inner upheaval, she couldn't help noticing that the house looked a little dishevelled. There was potential there though, in its high ceilings and harmonious lines. The sitting room was handsome enough, with pleasing antiques and several graceful lampshades casting warm pools of light, but the elegant, capacious sofa and the cushions on the comfortable-looking armchairs all looked as if they could do with a good plumping up.

She could tell which was Sebastian's favourite chair because his imprint was squashed into the cushions, and there was a space in the dust on the beautiful old coffee table between the laptop and numerous coffee mugs where two large male feet might comfortably rest.

The room had a neglected sort of comfort, as if someone with taste had started moving in, then been waylaid. She made for the safety of the sofa, hesitated, then gave the seat cushions a wipe before risking her suit.

Sebastian strolled in behind her with leisurely, confident calm, and at once her eyes zeroed in on the unmistakable fact that he'd taken off his jacket and waistcoat. In his shirtsleeves it was easy to see his lean angularity and the powerful outline of his shoulders.

He hesitated a moment, then to her relief made for his armchair, dropping into it and stretching out his long legs with idle ease.

Burningly aware of seeming like a craven coward, she attempted some light conversation. 'Er... Is this your primary residence, or just a beach villa?'

Amusement tinged his expression, but he replied with solemn politeness, 'Both. You get a better night-sky out here. Not that I'm always in residence. In recent months I've often needed to work so late I've found it easier to stay over at the office.'

'Oh.' She seized on the potential escape hatch and said eagerly, 'Well, if you'd rather do that tonight, don't you worry about me. I can look after myself.'

His brows shot up and his eyes gleamed. 'But it's your wedding night, Ariadne.'

She flashed him a brilliant smile. 'I know, but, heavens, I'm not so hung up on all those old traditions. If you need to go somewhere and do things with your satellites, go right ahead.'

His brows drew together, and he said silkily, 'There are *some* traditions that shouldn't be ignored.' His sexy, heavy-lidded gaze flickered over her face, and she realised she might have given away her very slight case of nerves.

A kiss, even a very hot kiss, was one thing, especially if it happened unexpectedly. A woman's natural instincts took over. But a wedding night was something else again. Something official, formal, that required a certain poise and graceful expertise. Should she inform him she was a virgin, or would he just take it for granted? She had no idea what his attitudes were about such things, though last night he'd clearly expected her to be free and easy about sex. What if she confessed her inexperience and he laughed?

She didn't think she could bear it if he laughed. There were some things a woman just couldn't discuss with a man.

She felt so naive and out of her depth. And the nervier she felt, the more relaxed and idle he seemed to become. Maybe he wasn't thinking about sex at all?

She met his dark gaze then and a major earthquake rocked her insides. A lazy, wicked smile was touching his mouth, and she was reminded of a big patient panther in the mood for play. He was thinking about it, all right.

'Now, what was it you wanted to talk about?' His black lashes had developed a sleepy languor. 'Can I get you something to help you relax? Some chocolate?'

'No. No, thanks. I—don't need to relax.' She got off the sofa and started pacing about, clasping her hands in front of her. 'Look, er, I'm not sure what you expect. I probably should explain that I'm...' She was just winding up to expand on the difficult subject when her foot connected with something on the floor. She tripped, only just managing to maintain her balance.

'Oh! Tsk.' She glared down in irritation at a thick heavy book entitled *Time Drag: Was Einstein Right?* lying where some lazy person had left it by Sebastian's armchair.

He sprang up. 'Sorry. That shouldn't be there.' He picked up the book and tossed it carelessly across the room onto a large pile stacked by an empty bookshelf. The pile collapsed and books scattered, sending up a mushroom cloud of dust.

Besides the heaps of unshelved books, she noticed several paintings on the floor leaning against the wall, and a couple of packing crates he was using to prop up his stereo system. Momentarily distracted, she enquired, frowning, 'How long since you moved in here?'

He shrugged. 'Oh, must be three years.' He glanced about as if for the first time, looking rueful. 'I guess I should have... I didn't have a chance to warn Agnes I'd be bringing you home tonight. There should be flowers. Oh, and I meant to... These ought to be shelved.'

He strolled across and gave the pile of books a desultory kick to shove them out of the way. More dust rose in the air.

'Sorry.' He gave an amused laugh. 'Agnes doesn't get time for the finer touches.'

She delved into her purse for a tissue, and held it to her face until the dust settled. 'How many staff do you have?'

'Just Agnes.'

'In *this* big house?' She arched her brows. 'Does Agnes have cooking duties as well?'

He looked evasive. 'Well, she has cooked, but...I don't often eat here, anyway. I'm sure we can get her to rustle up some meals.'

She felt curious to know what sort of relationship he had with his housekeeper if he wasn't certain he could persuade her to cook. 'Anyway,' she murmured, almost to herself, 'it doesn't matter. Really. I'm hardly going to be here long enough to notice.'

He turned and looked across at her, eyes glinting. Then he strolled back, determination in his smile. 'We'll see. No, no, not there, come and sit down here.' She'd been about to relocate to the strategic safety of the other armchair, but he drew her inexorably back to the sofa, and dropped down beside her.

'Now, what was it you wanted to chat about?' He lounged back, angling his body to face her, one arm resting along the sofa back behind her. Absently, almost unconsciously, he began to caress her cheek with his lean, tanned fingers. 'Was it something about your uncle and aunt?'

She felt a wary surprise. 'What about them?'

'Well, you seemed a little reluctant to have them at your wedding.'

'My *convenient* wedding.'

He smiled. 'I was surprised. I'd have thought you'd be pretty fond of them.' The touch of his fingertips on her cheek caused a delicious tingling that radiated to her ear and down her neck.

She lowered her lashes and crushed down the jagged spike in her private family emotional register. 'I am fond of them.'

'Aren't you the apple of their eyes?'

'Perhaps. Well, I was… *Thought* I was…' She smiled to cover the unwelcome pricking at the backs of her eyes. 'You can be mistaken about people. Even people you think you know very well.'

He shot her a keen glance, and she had the mortified feeling her voice might have given her away. She prayed he hadn't spotted the pathetic shimmer suddenly misting her vision. All at once she felt so weary, as if she were weighed down with all the miseries of the world. And she could feel the searchlight of his sharp intelligence probing her sad little secrets like a solar flare.

But he said quietly, 'Yeah, I guess. So…is there anything wrong over there with your family? Anything worrying you?'

As if she could tell him any of that. *Theos*, he'd done the trading deal with her uncle. They were probably in daily communication. Sure, Sebastian Nikosto looked reassuringly strong, and right now sympathetic and sincere, but he was the last person on the planet she could trust. No, the third last. *No, no*, she reflected with a dreary sigh. She'd been forgetting Demetri. Fourth last.

'Wasn't there something you wanted to tell me?'

She crashed back to earth. 'Oh, right. Well. I—I think we need to discuss… I think you know… You—you *should* know…' His fingers traced a soft searing trail down the side of her neck. Should she have stopped him? Though *he* might not have been conscious of it, she was. But it was only a caress, barely that. A harmless, friendly caress. It wasn't as if it were anything sexual.

'You do know this is just a marriage of convenience.' She swallowed. 'In fact…I—I'm not sure we're properly married at all.' She couldn't help closing her eyes briefly to savour the ongoing sensation. Her breath grew short and made her voice huskier than usual, her words disjointed. 'You must see…see that…in the eyes of the church, we…we haven't been properly joined.'

The smile gleamed in his eyes. 'That can very easily be fixed. We can be joined just as soon as you like.'

'*Oh.* You know what I mean. I'm not sure that we should— sleep together.'

He said very firmly, 'Yes, we should.'

'No, well…I'm a very light sleeper.' She searched his face in an attempt to gauge his reaction. 'I think I'll feel better if I sleep here on the sofa.'

'I don't think so.'

He stopped stroking her cheek, leaving her skin feeling bereft and yearning. *Aching* for him to start it again, she edged her cheek a little closer to him. With a grave expression, this time he stroked some hair back from her ear, then circled her ear with his fingertips.

Her entire being melted into swoon as thrills shivered through her scalp and down her spine.

'I think I can promise you'll feel much better if you sleep in the bed.' There was a suave, confident finality in his tone.

'No, what I'm trying to say is—that I'm not sure I feel married enough to—you know.'

'Make love?' he supplied, lifting his black brows and smiling like the very devil.

She gave a nod. 'Without the blessing of the church.'

'Oh, but…' his expression grew solemn '…what could be a holier place to wed than a garden? I have to say I felt *very* blessed.' He made an expansive gesture. 'There we were, at one with the earth, the sea and the sky, kissed by the rays of the setting sun.'

'Oh, well, *perhaps*…' Had there been some special deeper inflection in the way he said 'kissed', or had her hypersensitivity to the hot, strong current she sensed emanating from him made her imagine it? 'It was lovely, I know, but…' she had to give her conscience a proper hearing '…just because we're married doesn't mean we *should*.'

He pinned her with his compelling glance and said softly, and very definitely, 'No, my sweet wife, we *should* because I want you and you want me.'

She met his hot dark gaze and all her arguments dried on her tongue while her heart slithered into emergency pounding.

Suddenly he bent his head and planted a soft little kiss at the base of her throat. It was so thrilling and unexpected, she couldn't restrain a gasp. Then he trailed more kisses down her chest, all the way to the valley between her breasts. She felt them surge with warmth under the lapels of her jacket.

If only he would push her lapel aside and kiss her *there*. Imagining it sent a hot helpless rush to her nipples.

He smelled so attractively male, and his hot hungry lips on her skin ignited such arousing little fires, her breathing grew increasingly shallow. Still, she struggled to retain some control.

'All right, fine,' she panted after a second. Despite what Thea had said, she was quite willing to compromise. 'Perhaps…I *could* feel okay about a kiss.'

He drew back from her, leaving the skin he'd recently aroused ablaze with yearning for more.

'A kiss?' He considered it, scanning her face with a narrowed gaze. Then he nodded. 'Hmm. A kiss is fairly harmless. That shouldn't disturb your conscience too much.' He continued his meditative scrutiny for a while, then grinned, so wickedly her insides turned over and a hot hungry flame flared low in her abdomen. 'Anyway, since we've already kissed once, I guess that genie is out of the bottle now.'

'*Twice*.' She gazed at him from under her lashes. 'Remember? We've kissed—twice.'

His voice was darker than a cavern. 'I remember.'

The gleam in his eyes grew so piercingly sensual, she held her breath in suspense, her heart madly pounding. Then he brought his mouth firmly down on hers.

At first it was a fantastic collision of lips, until he took first her upper, then lower lip between his, sliding each one gently through his teeth as if for the maximum knowing of them.

*Theos*, it was *so* slow and sexy.

A heavy, voluptuous heat beat to her breasts, and she felt her nipples and other erogenous zones rouse to a moist yearning. Then his tongue slid into her mouth, tickling the delicate tissues inside and igniting little snakes of fire there that somehow wound their way through her bloodstream, inflaming her longing to be thoroughly stroked *everywhere*.

She found herself clinging to him. He deepened his possession of her mouth, his hot, wine-flavoured breath mingling with hers in intoxicating intimacy. Then she felt his hand slide under her lapel, and she felt him squeeze then gently caress her breast through the lace of her bra. Thrills shivered through her.

She was seized by the most urgent need to be rid of the bra, to allow her breasts to be free and bare to his clever, devouring hands. And all the while, down below between her legs, a wilder urgency burned.

Just when she felt all hot and afire, he broke the kiss and drew away from her. She dragged in some air, her skin tingling and crazy to be touched.

'There,' he said, his voice deeper than a growl. 'One kiss. How do you feel now?' His eyes were hot and slumberous, with a dark sexual flame that somehow exacerbated the hunger in her blood.

His shirt collar was unbuttoned, opening to a triangle of bronzed skin at the base of his strong neck. Her mouth watered with a sudden insane need.

'Fine. Just fine. Only… Who said it had to be just one?' Her voice was smokier than a Naxos taverna.

It was only a kiss, after all. Giving him little chance to protest, she placed her hands on his shoulders, and leaned forward to press her lips to that bare triangle. A tremor passed through him, delivering her a thrilled satisfaction. His skin had a faintly salty, masculine taste that was distinctly moreish to her hungry lips. With her breasts rising and falling in the upheaval of a new and heady exhilaration, she slipped undone the next couple of buttons of his shirt, revealing a deeper expanse of masculine chest.

A sultry pang roiled through her as her glance fastened on his alluring whorls of black chest hair, just begging to be explored. She bent her lips to his hot satin skin, then almost of its own volition her tongue licked a trail all the way to his neck. She felt another satisfying shudder rock him.

He grabbed her upper arms then and held her a little away from him, but her hunger wasn't appeased. In fact it intensified. Her avid gaze flicked to his mouth, and it was as though she couldn't help herself. She just *had* to.

She leaned forward and pressed her lips to his, feeling his thrilling leap of response, tasting and savouring and exploring with her tongue until she felt so hotly aroused with pleasure, she was aflame. Then he took charge of the clinch, his hands suddenly becoming rough and urgent to explore her willing curves. Her hands were infected with the same mad thirst. They couldn't keep from roaming, craving to feel his shoulders and powerful chest, sliding under his shirt to explore the lean hard contours of muscle and bone.

Somehow she found herself lying down, ablaze, her head on the cushions against the armrest, with Sebastian's long lean frame half lying on top of her. But it was still only kissing. Somehow they each adjusted their bodies, his so lean and angular, hers softer, more yielding, to find a way to kiss on the limited space without interrupting the steamy progress.

To her sinful delight, Sebastian was an expert at creating pleasure with his hands. She wasn't sure when her jacket became unbuttoned, but the kiss grew even hotter and sexier as his clever fingers stroked her yearning breasts and sent tingles resounding through her body.

Far too soon though, he broke from her. She waited, her momentary disappointment quickly changed by his scorching gaze to a limbo of thrilled suspense. What next? With a searing glance, he bent his lips to her breasts, and to her shock deliberately sucked each yearning nipple through the lace of her bra.

Ah-h-h, *bliss*. The gentle friction of the cloth and his mouth on her sensitive peaks was so arousing, her desire blazed to an inferno. Her convulsive fingers mauled his shoulders, kneaded his arms, tangled in his hair as she gasped and cried out in pleasure. Then just when she was ready to melt into a molten puddle, he drew away from her and sat up.

Panting, she eyed him hungrily. Far from being satisfied, her appetite to taste his kisses seemed to have escalated to an evil obsession.

'Come here,' she rasped throatily, surprised by her own boldness, half sitting in the attempt to grab him and pull him back to her.

But he placed a light but firm hand on her chest. 'Stay there.' His dark drawl rippled down her spine like the devil's breath. For a second he sat very still, the gleam in his eyes darker and more seductive than she'd yet observed.

Her blood seethed with the most delicious anticipation.

He made sure she was comfortable, arranging her cushions securely against the arm of the sofa, lifting her feet to rest on his thighs. A wild and pleasurable suspense fluttered inside her.

He caressed her feet absently for a moment, watching her face, then traced a lean hand along her leg to her knee. 'Ah, these gorgeous legs,' he growled, bending to kiss her knee.

It was so flattering. She bent her knees up to make it easier for him if he felt like kissing them again. And he did. Though next time, he kissed her *above* the knee, on the inside of her thigh.

Her excitement intensified.

He stroked her legs with increasingly long and sensual sweeps, his fingertips rousing fire wherever they connected with her willing flesh. How far would he dare to go? Then his caressing fingers slipped under her skirt and travelled softly, gently, all the way up to the silken skin at the top of her inner thigh. Close, so scintillatingly close, to the holy of holies.

It was explosively dangerous, it was hardly a kiss, but the sensations were so thrilling, what else could she do but give herself up to voluptuous enjoyment?

And all the time, while rivulets of sheer pleasure radiated through her flesh, a very short distance away, covered only by the delicate cotton of her pants, her most intimate, secret parts burned to be included in the orgy. In truth, *Theos* pardon her weakness, the closer his questing fingers roamed to the strictly forbidden zone, the more she ached for him to caress her there.

While he gazed at her, his hot, slumberous eyes as dark as Lucifer's, she looked back at him, knowing her own eyes must reflect the pleasure she was feeling, at the same time hoping he'd somehow read her desperate yearning.

Then all at once his traversing hand moved a little further afield. She tensed in anticipation. A low, throaty moan escaped her as with the most thrilling pleasure she felt his fingertips softly glide across the flimsy fabric of her pants.

Ah-h-h.

He caressed her, so lightly, so tenderly it was the purest chocolate, the sheerest rapture, it was the darkest, most sinful black magic.

She was gasping, moaning, hardly able to keep herself from writhing out of control, when all at once he nipped down her pants, leaving her utterly exposed.

For a second she stared at him in complete shock. He gazed on her naked triangle of dusky curls with a riveted gleam in his eyes, then with a bold, determined smile he changed position, unhesitatingly parting her thighs to expose her nakedness even further. Then he bent his dark head right there between her legs.

*Theos*, it was so *erotic*. Having laid her completely bare, he stroked his divine tongue across the sensitive, most secret yearning folds of her body, with exquisite artistry connecting with her sweet spot and sucking.

'Oh-h-h.' How could he have known? She shuddered in ecstasy as wave after wave of liquid pleasure roiled through her with every delicious, forbidden touch.

But that wasn't all. Strangely, while the rapture was white-hot and intense, somehow her hunger grew and grew, until she reached some kind of pitch of maddened erotic need. Just when she thought she must scream, he thrust his heavenly tongue inside her and flicked it around the tenderest, most yearning tissues of all. Her wild pleasure escalated to a dizzy, suspenseful pitch, then crashed into shards of exquisite relief.

It took her some seconds to recover. Sebastian waited, his eyes so wicked and aroused, his brows lifted in amused query for her comment.

'Oh,' she said, when her breathing had slowed enough for her to speak, her voice hoarse and deeper than the Katherine Gorge. '*That* kind of a kiss.'

Ignoring the scruples she'd already thrown to the wind, she contemplated him with enthralled appreciation, speculating on what other pleasures she'd read of that he might be equally expert in delivering.

'You know, Sebastian,' she panted, 'it's cramped here on this sofa. I might—sleep better in the bed.'

# CHAPTER NINE

SEBASTIAN contemplated his bride with satisfaction. Her passionate writhings on the sofa cushions had mussed her blonde hair into an enticing state of disarray, and her already full mouth was so plump and voluptuous from kissing, it was as much as he could do not to flatten her to the bed and devour her at once.

But unless he was mistaken, he had an instinct, unchanged by his initial lustful exploration of her honeyed flesh, that his proud bride was a virgin, a condition it would be his fiercest pleasure to correct, though tenderly, as befitted a princess on her wedding night.

She stood before him on the rug, eyeing the arrangement of the pillows on his bed. 'You know, Sebastian,' she said, with an uncertain laugh, 'I know I seem incredibly cool and casual about all this…negotiating this deal to marry you, then doing it all in a hurry, going through with the wedding and kissing you so…so…*often*. But the truth is…'

There was the faintest tremor in her voice, and he stilled in the act of tearing off his shirt. 'I can assure you,' he said, 'the linen's clean. It only came back from the Holy Cross Laundry this morning. Agnes was making the bed as I left.'

'Was she?' Ariadne frowned slightly. At least Agnes performed some part of her duties with passion. 'Where does Agnes sleep?'

'At her place,' he said, smiling.

She was about to question him further when she caught sight of the uninterrupted expanse of his gorgeous chest. Her mouth dried at the impressive proportions of his hard pectorals, his muscled arms.

'Goodness, you're very athletic,' she exclaimed. 'I hadn't realised quite how big you are.'

Startled into a grin, Sebastian let his shirt drop. Surprisingly, she'd rebuttoned her suit jacket after he'd carried her back in and deposited her on the rug, suggesting a back-pedalling in the momentum he'd so artfully established. Was his bride losing her nerve?

'Now,' he murmured, taking her arms and drawing her to him. 'Forget Agnes. You were saying something about the truth...?'

She closed her eyes. 'I—I think you understand that I won't be staying here long...'

Her brow was creased in worry, and he had a sudden inkling of the most immediate cause of her concern. He felt a rush of tenderness for her as she went on, 'You weren't hoping for a wife with the beautiful dark eyes, were you? Because, I truly think...'

He tilted up her face. 'Just relax,' he murmured. 'No need to think. Leave it all to me. Tonight is a night to feel.'

'But...' Ariadne was about to try again with her confession, when he took her mouth in a hotly demanding kiss. As his intoxicating flavour again invaded her senses, her overactive brainwaves, stressed by the rapid flow of events, calmed to a low, sultry purr.

She linked her arms around his neck and responded in kind, locked in like an electrocution victim to his high-voltage sexual power.

As she opened to him and she felt the virile length of his erection push against her abdomen, some primitive instinct tempted her to writhe her pelvis against him in sensual encouragement. The effect must have been potent, because the kiss intensified to a sizzling firestorm.

Drowning in tastes and sensations, compelled by the iron-hard demands of his big, masculine body, she clung to him, excited by his bronzed bare chest, his hot, roving hands, and wired to the thrilling beat of his big powerful heart against her breasts.

At last the kiss broke, leaving her panting and breathless, and hungry, oh, so hungry for more of him. His eyes were black, with a golden shimmer of lust tingeing the dark flame in their irises.

He set her a little away from him, watching her face as he undid her buttons one by one. Anxious now for skin contact, she wriggled out of the jacket and turned her back to allow him to unfasten her bra.

Slowly, gently, Sebastian traced the ridge of her spine with his thumb, feeling the electric quiver of response under her skin. His heart clenched at the beauty of her slim pale back. He located her skirt zip and drew it down, hardening in anticipation for the moment when she would be totally nude.

Ah. As smooth and delicately shaped as a violin.

His underwear tightened beyond endurance.

The skirt fell to the floor. She gave a small gasp, as if she'd forgotten she'd already lost her pants in the first round. The fierce blood beat a torrid path to his groin as his lustful gaze took in the graceful curves of her neck and waist, the delicious flare of her hips and smooth, satin bottom. He ached to plunge his burning length into her then and there, but with iron self-restraint merely bent to kiss the alluring dent in the small of her back, then turned her to face him.

Ariadne burned under his scorching regard of her nude body. Adrenaline, or desire, had dulled her anxiety. She felt bathed in a feminine glow, a primeval woman facing her mate.

He pushed her onto the bed, and she stretched out in the middle while he stripped off the rest of his clothes.

He was so beautifully made, a lean, bronzed, hairy symphony of muscle, sinew and masculine power, but when her eyes took in the massive extent of his thickly erect penis, her nerve jumped and she could almost feel herself shrink.

'I think I should tell you,' she quavered without further delay, 'I'm a virgin.'

'Yeah?' he said, smiling as he came down beside her with such tender warmth she felt her heart lurch. 'Who'd have guessed?'

Sebastian gazed down at his bride, her hair wild on the pillow, her luscious breasts with their raspberry-pink peaks straining for his attention, and his grin faded as he was seized with a solid-steel conviction that he wouldn't be letting her go any time soon.

'You're such a beautiful woman I can't believe some guy hasn't snapped you up,' he said, his voice so deep it was a primal growl from the earth's core. A shadow, so fleeting he might have imagined it, crossed her face, and he thought of what she'd told him about her past suitors. Someone had hurt her along the way.

She lowered her lashes, then smiled at herself with such shame and self-doubt he felt a sharp tug in his chest. 'It's me. I always choose the wrong ones.'

'Not this time,' he said with a fierce, tender certainty. 'This time you've chosen the right one.'

Ariadne felt shaken by the warmth and sincerity in his eyes, then as she continued to scrutinise him they flamed and all she could read in them was sizzling hot lust.

He bent his head, then softly, lightly ran his tongue-tip over her lips in a sexy little tease. Then he crushed her mouth in a fiery kiss, compelling her with the force of his passion to leave everything else behind, summoning her to this one moment in time and space.

Their hot breath rushed and mingled. As she lay in his powerful arms his chest hairs grazed her tender naked breasts, setting her skin alight with tingling little explosions of pleasure.

Possessed by his demanding lips, his hair-covered legs brushing her smooth skin, his rock-hard rod tickling her sex, she felt her veins flow with fire.

He broke the kiss first, in the nick of time to save her from drowning in sensation. But her body had sprung back to life with a primitive thirst that couldn't be ignored.

When he bent his head to her breast and took her nipple in his mouth, she mewled with pleasure. Then he explored her with his hands and lips until she was mindless and wild, a moaning, writhing creature incandescent with desire, a willing, wanton prey to a mutual, insatiable passion.

As the sensational storm raged she burned with a potent yearning. She tried not to obsess, but his arousal was so straight and strong and masculine, and in some way so *right*, springing from those crisp, little black curls, every fibre in her body was on edge.

At last Sebastian paused to take a foil packet from the bedside table. He tore it open, and she watched him slide the sheath onto his rosy, throbbing length, hoping against hope she would stretch half as well as the condom had. At the very thought she felt a tingling rush of moisture between her legs.

'Now,' he said, passion in his dark eyes. He parted her thighs, and traced the delicate folds until they felt as plump and full as a peach and she was reduced to a quivering, burning mess. Her need for release reached a desperate pitch.

'Sebastian,' she breathed shudderingly, arching up to him. 'I'm on fire here.'

With intense satisfaction in his hot eyes he slid a finger inside her. 'And you're tight,' he murmured, gently stretching the entrance to her moist channel, his voice like thick husky gravel. 'So fabulously tight.'

She wrinkled her brow. 'That's a good thing?'

'It's a *great* thing,' he said, then positioned himself between her legs and firmly pushed inside her. She felt filled to bursting point.

'*Theos*,' she cried, digging her fingers into his hard, muscled arms. '*Sebastian*.'

He withdrew at once, soothing her with his voice, 'Sweetheart, sweetheart,' he crooned, stroking her hair. 'It might be uncomfortable the first time. But it'll get better. Trust me.'

Trust him? He looked supremely confident, but there was a concerned little frown between his eyes. She had a vague realisation that he'd already given her one fabulous moment of blissful release. What about his? And did she really want to draw back after going this far down the road to losing her virginity?

She knew what to expect, after all. Her girlfriends had told her in graphic detail, and she'd read enough about how it would hurt. Clamping her eyes shut, she steeled herself to the agony. 'Go on, then. Get it over with.'

He bent to kiss her lips, then when she was least expecting it gave an almighty thrust, and she felt a raw little pinch that tore a pained gasp from her.

He froze all action, then withdrew from her, his face taut with concern. 'Are you okay?'

The smarting eased almost at once. 'Well, *now*.' She made a check of her bodily sensations, but could find no lingering pain. 'Is that it?' she said tensely. 'Just that?'

His anxious expression lightened and he smiled, while the dark flame smouldering in the depths of his eyes reached deep into her womb. 'That's just the beginning. Now it's the good part. Just relax.'

He eased into her again, and this time the sensation didn't feel quite so strange.

'See how we go, Ariadne Giorgias.' He watched her face, a sexy little smile edging up the corners of his mouth as he started to move his lean hips, stroking inside her with seductive, sinuous little movements that weren't as uncomfortable as she'd expected.

'How does that feel?' he said huskily, his eyes tender and

warm and desirous. 'I'm inside you, and you're opening to me…' He eased her into a gentle rhythm. 'Like a glove. A beautiful tight, hot, velvet…' His scorching hot eyes flared and he increased the rhythm. At first it just felt athletic and very intimate, but then every so often, amazingly, she felt his hard rod touch some spot inside her that ignited like a sunburst, sending streaks of the most intense and fabulous pleasure throughout her entire body.

'Go on,' she urged, wanting more of them. 'Go *on.*'

He rocked her even faster, then she could tell by his increasingly concentrated expression that he'd become locked in a rapture of his own. She let go of her fears and gave herself up to the rhythm entirely, each stroke igniting more and more pleasure points inside her until she was a river of blissful sensations.

She wrapped her legs around him, relishing all the physical sensations of his hard, lean masculinity, the intimacy and warmth of the amazing connection.

Feeling his hard, sensitised flesh swell with unbelievable bliss inside her slickly tight sheath, Sebastian gritted his teeth with the sublime pleasure.

Locked in his arms, Ariadne strove faster and faster, harder and higher, until before she knew it he was once again zooming her up that wild, hot, delicious incline to an even higher, more glorious summit than before. She hung there in a desperate trembling suspense, then her moment came and she dissolved into waves of ecstatic, rapturous pleasure.

'Oh, *Theos,*' she gasped as the ripples subsided.

Sebastian reached a climax of his own, then collapsed upon her, his lean bronzed body sheened with sweat. After a few seconds he lifted himself off her and rested quietly with his eyes closed. Then he hauled himself up and went into his bathroom. She lay bathed in a slumberous glow, her body purring in relaxation while she listened to the flow of the taps.

Soon he came back and stretched out beside her with his eyes shut. She'd started to think he'd fallen asleep, when he rolled on his side to face her. He smiled down at her, his warm gaze a mixture of triumph and tenderness, reaching out to trail a gentle finger over her shoulder and along the line of her body.

'I'd have thought you might have at least said, "Oh, *Sebastian*."'

She gave a low throaty laugh. 'Sorry. You *were* good.'

'Thank you,' he said modestly.

She smiled into his eyes. 'My aunt told me you were a genius.'

His deep laugh rumbled, then he planted a little kiss on her breast. 'From this point on, we only get better.'

'With practice, you mean?' She fluttered her lashes at him. 'How much practice?'

'Plenty,' he growled. Then he grinned and pulled her into his arms. 'Aren't you glad we got married?'

After a while, in which she floated in a sort of dreamy glow, relaxed and intimate in the soft dark, he said, 'So what happened with that guy? The one who broke your heart?'

'I didn't say that.'

'As good as.'

Had she, though? She thought back to the night before. She'd said so many things at that restaurant. She must have been out of her head. Still, here and now in the most intimate and blissful cocoon she'd ever been wrapped in, honesty had never felt safer.

'Demetri Spiros,' she said after a while. 'I was engaged to him.'

'*Engaged?*' He sounded astonished.

'Well, it was one of those things. I met him on this cruise on Thio's yacht. You know how it can happen. *My* family wanted it, *his* family wanted it. He seemed really cool. Anyway, I found out he had a girlfriend in Athens. This older woman.'

'Older than him?'

'No, older than *me*. A few days before the wedding I saw him with her in a restaurant. She was really sophisticated. People said he would drop her after the wedding, once he had me, but I couldn't forget about it.' Some of the remembered pain must have leaked through into her voice, because he squeezed her a little tighter. 'Then on the wedding day when I was all dressed up in my white dress, I couldn't force myself to go through with it.'

'Hell. What did you do?'

'When they were all rushing about busy with things, I went down to the beach and stayed there all day, in my dress and everything. *Ruined* the shoes.'

'Your aunt and uncle would have been upset.'

Her stomach clenched with the old guilt, then she sighed. 'Oh, yes. Well, the whole world was there waiting in the church. I can't really blame them. Prince Philippos. The King and Queen of Sweden. The Grimaldis.'

He made a silent whistle. 'My God. All hell must have broken loose.'

In the dark, still bathed in the afterglow of passion, confession was easier. 'It was in all the papers. Thio said he was ashamed to walk down the street. Thea cancelled all her committees. And I lost my job. The gallery said I was too controversial.'

There was a long silence, though it felt warm and uncritical. His arms tightened around her and she felt his big strong heart beating against hers. Then his deep, comforting voice murmured in her ear, 'That guy was a damn fool. Fancy wrecking his chance with *you*.' He kissed her ear. 'I'm glad you did it, though. That took real courage. You're the bravest girl I ever met.'

After all the recriminations she'd suffered, the words were a soothing balm to her tortured soul, and she felt a flow of joyous relief. Her heart swelled with love for Sebastian Nikosto.

Ridiculous, maybe, stupid, obviously, but she was in love.

# CHAPTER TEN

ARIADNE couldn't stop smiling. She had a secret. A secret other women shared and only discussed with the dearest friends of their bosoms. Of course, everyone said sex was wonderful. But how could she have guessed how delicious, how comforting it would be to sleep in the arms of a big, warm man?

Privately, she doubted if those other women's experiences came even close to the pleasure she'd discovered sleeping with Sebastian. They might think their men were fantastic, but it was hard to believe theirs could be as tender, or as fierce and clever. And beautiful. Why hadn't she seen before how truly beautiful men could be?

There'd been more heavenly love during the night, with Sebastian taking such gentle care not to hurt her, and he'd said some wonderful things she'd treasure in her heart for ever.

Sebastian must have been an early riser, because when she woke soon after dawn he wasn't there. He'd come back a little later, glistening wet from an early morning surf to shower and get ready for work. He seemed silent at this time of day, stern and rather brooding. Nothing like the midnight Sebastian. She sensed it might be best to absent herself while he prepared for the office, so she put on his silken robe and wandered giddily out on the balcony to view the surroundings through her dreamy, love-drunk haze.

And such surroundings. The balcony doors opened to a panoramic view of the Pacific Ocean, with long lines of breakers rolling in to foam on the long sandy beach below the villa. To either side of her more expensive villas and apartment blocks clung to the headland, squeezed in with older, more modest dwellings and charming little shops and restaurants. Stairs from Sebastian's terraced garden carved a steep narrow path down to the beach walk, where even at this early hour dozens of people strolled or jogged to revel in the bracing sights and smells.

Below the balcony was a sparkling pool, its azure waters cunningly positioned to suggest a cascading effect from pool to ocean. The garden was a little overgrown, though in a leafy corner a lounger and an umbrella table were set up among the weeds with a certain charm.

It wasn't Naxos, but how would she ever leave it?

She heard Sebastian's step behind her and turned, smiling. He was fresh with masculine soap and aftershave.

'Oh, well, I'm off now.' He bent to brush her cheek with his lips.

Her heart panged. 'So early?' She'd hoped he might think it important to spend time with her, but she didn't want to cling like a needy housewife.

He looked so darkly desirable in his crisp white shirt and business suit, she felt a glow of pride. Legally he belonged to her, at least for the moment. In fact it felt like a risk to let him out of her sight. Amazingly, Jenny, his PA, hadn't seemed to be in love with him, but there were other women in the workplace, women who must notice his incredible sexiness.

Unable to help herself, she made a slight adjustment to his shirt collar. He barely gave her time to finish before he detached himself and stepped away from her.

'Oh, I've got the marriage certificate here,' he said, patting his pocket. 'I'll fax it from the office, if that's all right with you?'

'Oh. Oh, good. That's fine.'

He sounded so brisk and efficient. Was she imagining it, or was he avoiding meeting her eyes? In no time it seemed he was heading downstairs for the door.

'What? No coffee? No breakfast?' she couldn't prevent herself from calling after him in a last bid to keep him.

He arrested his stride and half turned. 'There's stuff in the fridge, I think.' Then his eyes narrowed. 'Er... Now that I think of it, you might want to go down to one of the cafés. I'll catch something in the city.' He hesitated as if he wanted to say something more, then seemed to think better of it. 'Well...anyway... have a great day.' With a backward wave over his shoulder he strode for the door.

Was he so eager to get to his satellite designs? It gave her a bit of a cold burr. She couldn't imagine Thea allowing Thio Peri to leave for his office without sharing breakfast with her.

Disappointed, she turned back inside and gave her bath a careful rinse, then filled it and climbed in for a long, hot soak in the rosemary-scented bath bubbles she'd brought from Naxos.

In truth, she was sore, though it was a good and useful soreness. The sort that came from having given and received the most bounteous of pleasures as a warm and passionate woman. A real woman, at last. She kept wanting to hug herself with the precious knowledge of her new self.

Fresh-scented and relaxed after her bath, she applied some soothing moisturiser to the areas most affected, then slipped on a tee shirt and went downstairs to investigate the kitchen. There was hardly anything in the fridge, apart from a number of plastic containers holding strange-looking leftovers, and a few bottles of beer. She sniffed a tub of ancient yoghurt and wrinkled her nose in disgust. Nothing like the yoghurt at home. The freezer, on the other hand, was packed with frozen dinners.

No fresh fruit. No vegetables or salad, and where was the coffee? Who could survive on such food?

Postponing the problem, she drifted back upstairs and

crawled into the bed to luxuriate in recollections of every fantastic thing Sebastian had done to her, and the gorgeous things he'd said. Every time she thought of how warm his eyes had been her insides swirled. With a twinge she wondered if it was natural of him to have retreated into himself and become rather remote this morning. Perhaps he simply wasn't a morning person.

She was just drifting into a blissful doze when she was startled back into wakefulness by sounds in the house. Someone was downstairs. Sebastian?

She bounded out of bed and flew down the stairs, only to be brought up short by the sight of a large grey-haired woman in the hall, bucket and mop beside her as she propped herself up against the wall and inhaled from an asthma puffer.

The woman started with surprise when she saw Ariadne. She finished dosing herself and slipped her puffer into the pocket of her capacious overall. 'Oh, heck,' she wheezed. 'I didn't know anyone was here.'

'Hello,' Ariadne said, smiling. 'Agnes, is it?'

'That's right, love. I…' Agnes broke off again to breathe deeply. 'Sorry. I just have to catch me breath.' After a few heavily breathing seconds she inspected Ariadne with curiosity. 'You must be a friend of Seb—Mr Nikosto.'

Ariadne nodded, noting that Agnes's face had a high unhealthy colour, as if from major exertion. She held out her hand. 'Ariadne.'

She'd been about to say Ariadne Giorgias, but wasn't quite sure where she stood with that now. She clasped Agnes's rather clammy hand with some concern. 'Are you feeling quite well, Agnes? Would you like to sit down and have a cup of tea?'

'Oh, no, love. I'll be fine in a while. It's just me asthma. It's this humid weather. I'm all right if I don't have to do anything too strenuous. Times like this I just do a bit here and there, and wait for a good day so I can fix up the rest.' She wheezed in a few breaths, then added, eyeing Ariadne's tee shirt and bare legs, 'Staying here, are you?'

Her eyes lit up when Ariadne nodded. 'Good, good. It's about time. Don't like to see a good man go to waste.' She grinned.

Ariadne smiled uncertainly. 'Fine. Well, thanks, Agnes. I'll just…' She gave a little wave and turned for the stairs.

Agnes bent to pick up her bucket, talking and puffing at the same time. 'That's okay. Just leave it with me, love. Though I don't think I'll be making it up the stairs today.'

Ariadne walked back up, thinking fast. That bucket looked heavy. Poor Agnes needed help. A villa of this size really needed more staff to do it justice. Sebastian hadn't seemed very concerned about it last night, though, of course, he'd had other things on his mind. She smiled in recollection of those other things.

Still, if she'd been in charge here, she'd have enjoyed bringing the chaos into order and making everything shine, showing him how comfortable and beautiful his home could be. Heavens, she was even starting to think like a wife. Thea would be so proud to see her life's work paying off. She grimaced.

A little later she descended again, clad in jeans and a shirt. Agnes was in the dining room, supporting herself by leaning with both hands on a chair back while she caught her breath. She gave Ariadne a wave, clearly unable to speak.

Ariadne took one look at the suffering woman and was inspired, partly by her conscience. 'How would it be, Agnes, if I gave you a helping hand?' Agnes's mouth dropped open, but she insisted. 'Come on. Where do you keep all your cleaning potions?'

Vacuuming was strenuous work, Ariadne discovered, and so was washing floors, dusting and polishing. Domestic work had clearly been underrated as an exercise regime. But she'd never have guessed what satisfaction there was in personally being the one to make surfaces gleam and bring the subtle glow of cleanliness to rooms that had formerly been dull and dusty. She could hardly wait to see the surprise and pleasure in Sebastian's eyes when he came home that evening and saw his villa looking bright and neat and shiny.

Agnes managed some dusting in the downstairs rooms, and, though she'd been worried to be assisted at first, now she seemed grateful to have the load of responsibility shared. In a mounting frenzy of domestic enthusiasm Ariadne attacked the bathrooms with sponges, scrubbing brushes and fresh-smelling germicidal sprays.

Windows, she mused, standing with her hands on her hips to survey her handiwork. Should she clean windows? *Theos*, married a day and she'd turned into a housewife. If Naxos could see her now!

Agnes went home early to rest, to Ariadne's secret relief.

After several athletic hours she changed into fresh clothes and prepared to solve the food problem. If she was to stay in Bronte a few days, for those few days she would try to somehow alter the breakfast situation to eat with Sebastian. Perhaps outside on the kitchen deck? By the pool? In bed?

Her insides flipped over when she thought of bed, then she experienced a tinge of regret. Bed might have become a whole new universe of excitement and delight, but it was one that couldn't last.

It was a pleasant downhill walk to the shops. People greeted her and said, 'Good morning,' several elderly souls stopping to chat about the weather. Exactly like Naxos. Among the restaurants she found a café with Danish pastries and quite good coffee. Disappointingly, their orange juice was the same fake stuff she'd been given at the airport and elsewhere.

There was a busy little delicatessen, with a fruit shop attached. She managed to fill a trolley, though remembering the hotel experience this time she carefully tallied the prices as she went. Feta and Greek yoghurt—so they *said*—eggs and bacon and tomatoes, in case Sebastian liked Australian breakfasts. Cereal to cover all contingencies. Olives and filo pastry, although she couldn't find any real myzithra cheese to bake inside the layers, and had to make do. Italian coffee beans, tea from India. Oranges, honey and pine nuts, spinach and salad vegetables, and the best olive oil available, though it wasn't Greek.

And what about Sebastian's dinner? she thought with a surge of excitement. A man needed a nourishing diet. Simple Greek food, Thea always said, was the best in the world. Ideas for the dishes she might cook crowded into her head.

In the end she had to negotiate with the shop proprietor to deliver all the supplies to the villa. Delivery cost only a little more, though luckily she'd be getting her inheritance in a few days, because her funds were now quite alarmingly low.

After the walk back, she found the boxes of groceries ready and waiting on the doorstep. Excellent. She braced herself. Time to attack the kitchen and make it fit for haute cuisine.

Sebastian closed the Thursday meeting, conscious of the worried faces of his colleagues. Athens would be sleeping at this time, so, although he'd sent the proof of his marriage first thing, it would be several hours before he heard from Peri Giorgias and could relay the good news. His team deserved something to cheer them up.

When the contract came through, signed, sealed and delivered, he'd give everyone a substantial pay rise, extra time off and a bonus for their work on the Giorgias project. In the meantime...

In the meantime, he was glad when the seemingly excruciatingly long meeting was over and he could concentrate on the issue possessing his soul.

He'd married a woman. *Another* woman. A beautiful, sexy woman was in his house, waiting and available.

Every so often his conscience tried to throw in sly glimpses of Esther towards the end to torture him, her eyes and cheeks sunken, her skin like paper, but replays of the previous night had stormed in to dominate his head-space. Throughout the entire day he'd found himself stopping every so often and closing his eyes so he could savour the stirring images. Ariadne's lovely body, her smooth satin limbs. Her blue eyes, heavy-lidded and languorous in the lamplight, with that devastating mixture of naivety and arousal.

So trusting, so—*giving*. Her sensual beauty had promised passion, and he hadn't been disappointed. Far from it. She'd surrendered herself to him with total generosity and he'd immersed himself in her until his senses were saturated with her. And still he'd craved more.

While afterwards… His thoughts kept straying to her sweet low voice confessing her secrets in the dark. No wonder she'd seemed fragile, after that painful wedding scandal. Again she'd managed to pierce his emotional armour to move him. He'd felt such a fierce need to protect her, to hold her to him, and…

He clenched his fists. For God's sake, what was he *doing*? His *wife*, his true love only three years in the ground, and here he was lusting after another woman, imagining he was feeling things, emotions his conscience told him he had no right to feel.

In a rational sense he could diagnose the situation, of course. He'd been working too hard. Worrying too much about the crisis. Add to that having been deprived of feminine company for some time, it was only natural his senses should have woken up with such a vengeance. He was in the middle of a firestorm, and he'd just have to douse the flames.

Unless, of course, he could think of some safe way to ride them out?

No, it was clear the only way to deal with these few days would be to hold Ariadne Giorgias at arm's length. Already she was creeping into his mind, twining herself around his emotional nerve centre like some sort of addictive drug. It wasn't as if she were even his choice. The less he saw into her and her little issues, the better.

His last glimpse of her this morning flashed into his mind.

She'd looked so utterly desirable wrapped in the overlarge robe, her hair all in a tangle. The surprise in her eyes when he'd been a little curt with her had somehow twisted its way into his guts and stayed with him all the way into the city. But he needed to make it clear to her nothing had changed. Having sex meant nothing more than that. Sex, pure and simple.

Ms Giorgias needed to understand. She was temporary. Esther, *Esther* was the lodestar of his life.

He couldn't help wondering, though, what Ariadne would be doing with herself all day out at Bronte. How did a princess kill time in an empty house? He'd actually considered phoning her at various stages to see if she was all right, but thank God he'd conquered that weakness. Would he have been able to trust himself not to rush home and bed her all over again?

The strange look Jenny had given him when he'd bowled in this morning earlier even than the usual time flicked into his head, and he frowned to himself. Jenny should stick to worrying about her job.

As knock-off time approached people said their goodbyes and hurried off to their homes and families. The building gradually grew quiet. Lights started flickering on all over the city, but he didn't bother with his desk lamp. The dark made for better brooding, and he needed to get his head around things.

Esther's life and joy had been snatched away from her. God forgive him for the selfish bastard he was, but he had to grit his teeth and acknowledge the truth about himself at last. Shameful, despicable, but he'd actually felt relief when her dreadful battle was over and she was gone.

He heard the cleaners' cheerful clatter, then even that diminished. He stayed frozen at his desk, trying not to imagine the vivid woman at home, his soul in a vice.

Ariadne checked the oven for the umpteenth time. The potatoes looked scrumptious, and the aroma of the resting lamb reminded her it had been a long time since lunch. The salad had been sitting there ready for some time, and a simple *avgolemono* soup simmered fragrantly on the stove. She hoped Sebastian was hungry.

She'd unearthed a cloth, and set the dining table with silver and the only glasses she could find. In the absence of flowers she'd picked a leafy spray from a shrub in the garden.

She looked anxiously at her watch. Nearly nine. She remembered him saying he didn't always come home for dinner, but he would tonight, surely? Maybe she should call him. She gave him another twenty minutes, then headed for the study.

Sebastian's study was surprisingly well organised and quite atmospheric, with books neatly tucked into their shelves, and, on the walls, huge, glowing maps of star constellations to vie with the evening sky visible through the wide windows. At some point he must have intended to work in here, she thought, preparing to dial his mobile number. Her eye fell on a framed photo and she stood stock-still.

It was of Sebastian, on the steps of a church with a bride. A red-hot needle jabbed Ariadne's chest in that initial instant of shock, and her wild heart revved up for a few pounding seconds, so that she had to sit down until her brain caught up with her body.

So, he was married. *Had* been, she presumed, since he didn't seem at all like the sort of guy to commit bigamy. Although what did she know of him, really?

When her heart had slowed down she studied the picture. He was quite a bit younger there, his handsome face split with his gorgeous white grin. The bride was quite lovely too, she supposed. Dark-haired, although clearly not Greek. *She* didn't have the big, dark shining eyes, either. They had that look people in love had, joy and euphoria pouring from every pixel.

Ariadne's heart suffered another jab as she noticed his arm around the woman's waist. How silly though. How absurd to feel jealous about something she knew nothing about.

Where was his wife now? If they'd divorced, would he have kept a wedding photo on his desk as if he cherished it? Cherished *her*?

Ridiculous maybe, but she hesitated to phone him now, as if that would be presuming an intimacy she had no right to claim. She grimaced. Might as well face it. He wasn't coming home.

Feeling deflated, she went back to the kitchen and turned off all the heating rings. All at once then the exertions of the day seemed to catch up with her and she nearly buckled to a wave of fatigue. She surveyed the kitchen in despair. Now there was the problem of what to do with all the lovely food she'd prepared. At home, she'd have simply handed the kitchen over to someone else to restore after she'd cooked a meal, but here...

Here, she was on her own.

It took longer than she'd expected, deciding on suitable storage containers, packing it all into the fridge, then clearing the utensils, scrubbing the roasting pan and wiping down the surfaces to remove all signs of her idiotic endeavour. She paused to wipe her forehead on her sleeve. How could anyone even *want* to be a wife? It was just unremitting hard labour, and what was the point? To make a man happy when he couldn't care less?

What an absolute fool she'd made of herself, trying to act the part when she was only a temporary arrangement. A business deal.

Even so, as she hauled her exhausted self up the stairs an hour later she couldn't help thinking he *could* have come home to be with her. After those things he'd said to her last night, after he'd made love to her so passionately, being ignored just didn't feel right.

# CHAPTER ELEVEN

SEBASTIAN let himself quietly in his front door. It was nearly midnight, the house dark and silent. His nostrils twitched at an unusual scent in the air, like furniture polish mingled with the sort of clean household smells his mother's place always had.

For some reason he hesitated to switch the lights on, and when he walked quietly up the stairs found himself tempted by an absurd desire to take his shoes off. But why should he, for God's sake? It was his house.

There was no light on in his bedroom, and he blundered into a chest of drawers. He stilled, wincing, waiting for some reaction, but there was none. With a sharp lurch in his gut he realised there was no sleeping woman in the room. A sensation bordering on panic speared through him, and he hastened to switch on the lamps. Had she packed up and gone? Left him, for God's sake, even before he could get to know her properly?

In the lamplight the bed was smooth and untroubled. Then through the half-open door of her dressing room he glimpsed a corner of what looked like a suitcase. He sprang to push the door open further and with a flood of almost overwhelming relief saw that her clothes were there, hanging in the closet.

So, still in residence. He closed his eyes and let out a long breath. Not in his bed, where he'd expected, but some sort of tautness he sensed pricking in the atmosphere suggested she was almost certainly nearby. With questions clamouring in his brain he walked quietly along the hall, opening doors, and stopped short, his triumph mingling with bemusement when he discovered her sleeping form in the room across from his. At least, in the spill of light from the hall she *looked* as if she was asleep.

He paused, his hand on the doorknob, listening for her breathing.

'Ariadne?'

After a long, somehow nerve-racking moment, she stirred. 'Yes?'

Something about that husky *yes* confirmed his suspicions she hadn't really been asleep. She'd been lying there, listening for him. The question then arose as to *why* she wasn't in his bed. A guilty possibility sprang forcibly to mind, but he rejected it utterly. No, he'd done nothing wrong. Everything was good. Let her sleep alone if that was what she preferred.

'Er...' He took a few steps into the room, seized by a sudden concern. 'Did you manage to get some dinner?' In the dim light from the hall he could see she was on her side, her pale hair flowing loose, her smooth, bare shoulder exposed by the down-turned sheet.

'I wasn't very hungry, thanks.'

'Right. Okay. Look, er...sorry. Sorry I'm so late. I was—held up.'

There was no reply, and he tried another tack. 'Feel like a beer?'

'No.' She pulled the covers higher, and settled deeper into her sleeping position in what was clearly a dismissal.

He shrugged, backed out, then strolled downstairs. In point of fact, this cool statement of independence was a relief. It was better he didn't sleep with her. Wasn't that what he'd decided? Sleeping with her could only escalate his addiction, then how would he manage when she left?

The kitchen looked and smelled somehow different, the tiles seeming brighter and shinier, though it had been so long since he'd really noticed the room it could have just been his imagination. He opened the fridge door and stared in surprise. The shelves were packed with food. Genuine food. Fresh milk, oranges, leafy green things poking from the vegetable crisper. He investigated a large plastic container dominating the middle shelf and was astonished to find a roasted joint. He tore off a bit and tasted it. Despite being cold, it was as tender, succulent and delicious as anything his mother kept in her fridge.

He investigated further and found other containers: salad, potatoes sprinkled with oregano, some sort of herb sauce. And he was starving, he realised. He'd been so engrossed in contemplation at the office he hadn't thought to order in dinner. Without wasting any more time he took down a plate and served himself hearty portions of the leftovers, then sat at the kitchen counter and wolfed it all down, along with occasional sips of beer, thinking deeply as he ate.

She could cook. Who'd have thought it? The kitchen had been pulled into sparkling order, he could see, with the sort of attention to detail that had never been poor Agnes's strong point. He owed her his thanks, that much was certain, though why she must transfer to another bed was curious.

It wasn't bothering him exactly, but he had to admit it had come as a shock. If she was *tired*, if she wanted to sleep, she could have done that perfectly well in his bed. He was a civilised guy. He was hardly a gorilla, unable to keep his hands off her. He'd have made no demands on her, if that was what she truly wanted.

Maybe it had simply been the steamy summer night that had made her decide it would be more comfortable to sleep alone. That bare shoulder he'd glimpsed suggested she might have been wearing next to nothing.

He frowned. Surely she realised state-of-the-art air-conditioning was available at the flick of a switch. Maybe he needed to inform her of it. Encourage her back to her rightful place with a little tender persuasion.

Though ashamed of such a backsliding thought, he couldn't deny another rueful reflection. However proud and icy Ms Ariadne Giorgias might try to be, whether she knew it or not, persuading her into his arms would be so meltingly, deliciously easy for a sinful male animal like himself. He could start with kissing her throat…

He gave his jaw a thoughtful rub. Of course, if he intended anything like that, the considerate thing for him to do would be to shave.

He finished his meal and pushed his plate away, then, unusually for him, something about the clean state of the surfaces impinged on his brain. He rose and made an unprecedented effort to rinse the plate in the sink. God, if he wasn't careful he'd be turning into a metrosexual. Then his thoughts switched to her lying upstairs, possibly naked. No. No, he wouldn't. No chance of that.

He shrugged off his lascivious thoughts and made an effort to recapture the mood of resistance that had sustained him at the office. He'd embrace this opportunity to sleep alone. He could use it as a test of his endurance. Though he might have to resort to taking some good scientific reading material up with him to send him off to sleep.

He started for the study, but as he passed through the dining room something caught the periphery of his vision and he checked.

Oh, God. Oh, *no*. The dining table was set. Charmingly, intimately set for two. If Esther had been able to see that. He stared at it, aghast, then something about the brave little optimistic bunch of leaves in the middle of the table hit him like a punch in the chest.

He closed his eyes. Bloody hell, how dumb could a selfish bastard get?

The enormity of his day's behaviour swept through him in a tidal wave, and he stood for a minute, paralysed.

On the floor above, Ariadne lay thinking about the pathetic lies men told. Held up at work. *Who* needed to stay at work until midnight? Prime ministers, maybe. Presidents, just possibly, although she couldn't see Michelle Obama allowing it to happen too often. But CEOs? She strained her ears for sounds from below. There'd been a bit of clattering, followed by silence. Then suddenly she heard Sebastian bound up the stairs. She tensed as his energetic step rang out in the hall and inexorably, for the second time, approached her bedroom door.

'Ariadne?' he said softly. 'Are you awake?'

She frowned. 'Well, I am *now*.'

He advanced into the room. 'Look…I'm sorry I didn't manage to make it home for dinner. I didn't realise you'd cooked a meal.'

'That's all right,' she said at once. 'I know you didn't know.'

'I guess I should have thought,' he floundered. 'I didn't…er… I should've…'

'It really doesn't matter. What's a bit of food?'

'Oh, look. Look, sweetheart…'

He advanced a little further into the room and hovered there a moment. The air throbbed with sexual vibrations. Though her lids were shut tight she could feel his eyes devouring her. She clutched the sheet to her breast, fighting her own weak desire for him to tear it away.

'Do you mind…?' She could hear the smile in his voice. 'Can I just turn on this lamp?' She felt the side of the bed depress as he sat down.

'What do you think you're doing?' she said sharply, blinking in the sudden light.

His smile flashed. He'd undone his tie and it was hanging loose. In his shirtsleeves with his five-o'clock shadow, he was so stirringly handsome her insides melted dangerously, and her treacherous body suddenly felt alive and wanton with desire.

His voice was as smooth as butter. 'I just wanted to thank you for cooking that delicious food. I don't think I've ever had such a great meal in this house.'

'It was greater five hours ago.'

'Oh, I know, I know. It must have been. You're a fantastic cook.'

'I'm just an ordinary *plain* cook, Sebastian.' She could feel the warmth of his knee touching her through the sheet, and piled up the pillows so she could lean up on them and not be at a disadvantage.

'Oh, no, you're not. Not ordinary. And not plain. Certainly not plain.' His dark eyes were smouldering in that way she recognised, drifting to the plunging bodice of her pretty satin nightie with the rosebuds on it and the thin straps.

'Thank you, you're very kind,' she said coldly, sweeping down her lashes, 'but I hope you don't think I cooked that food on your account. I just happen to have been brought up to prefer nourishing home-cooked meals myself.'

'Of course, of course.' He nodded. 'And it *was* nourishing. Thank you. Oh, well.' He got up and casually stretched. His shirt tautened to the max and she noticed a little gap appear in the opening just above his belt buckle. 'I'm heading for the shower.'

Paradoxically, she felt an almost overwhelming disappointment. Didn't he want to at least try to overcome her resistance? She'd had some wonderful things lined up to say about being a chattel, a convenient sex-slave and a domestic workhorse.

He made it to the door, and before she could stop herself she said, 'I think you might have at least mentioned you were married.'

He froze, then turned to her, a strange rigidity in the movement. 'I *was* married,' he said coolly, something a little scary in his voice. 'But it has nothing to do with anything here.'

He walked away, and she was left feeling rebuked, her imagination running riot. Anything *here* obviously referred to her. *Theos*, she regretted ever mentioning it. How could she have been so brash?

She switched off the lamp and lay there in the dark, listening to the sounds of the shower across the hall, her brain racing. All right, so his life had nothing to do with her. But she had some rights, didn't she? Even as a temporary wife? All her good instincts about last night, and making love and feeling that fabulous current of connection with him, seemed to have been cut off. But why? What had she done wrong?

Was it something she'd said this morning?

The water stopped flowing, and eventually everything fell silent, though it was a deafening sort of silence, filled with vibrations. She wished she could go to sleep, but she had a big aching lump in her chest. Her husband had wanted her once and once only, it seemed. Even as a temporary wife she was a failure. She could never go back to Naxos. Her aunt and uncle were fed up with her, and she was a stranger in her own country.

She was lying there in the unfriendly alien dark, realising she had nowhere in the world to belong, when the silence was shattered by a ringing phone. It stopped almost at once. She guessed Sebastian must have answered it. In a little while he opened her door and put his head in.

'It's your uncle. He wants to talk to you.'

'No.' Emotion welled in her throat and she turned away and covered her head with the sheet.

'But—I really think you should talk to him. He sounds very concerned. He says your aunt's frantic with—'

That cut her to the quick. '*You* talk to him,' she said through the sheet. 'He's your friend.'

'He's not my friend,' he said tersely, then walked away, speaking into the phone, his voice grim. 'Look, Giorgias, it's late here. Ariadne can't come…'

After a few minutes he came back to her door and said more

calmly, 'He's left the name of the solicitors in the city who manage your trust. You need to make an appointment to see them, and they'll arrange the transfer of your inheritance.'

She didn't answer, and he came up to the bed, frowning, his hands opened in query. 'Look, whatever it is that's happened between you and them, can't you—?'

'No, I can't.' Her voice gave away her emotional state. Or the way she was lying all hunched up in the foetal position with the sheet bunched to her chest. It must have, because he lowered his big frame to the bed, his eyes warm with concern, his voice gentle.

'Oh, sweetheart…'

Oh, she was a weak fool, but he shouldn't have said that. Sympathy was always her undoing, and she already had a very tenuous hold on her control. Tears rushed into her eyes and she was forced to surreptitiously dab at them with the sheet.

'Oh-h-h, no. No.' He reached and grabbed her, taking her into his strong arms, holding her against his bare chest, murmuring soothing things to her while he stroked her hair, planting little kisses on her face and throat and shoulders.

'I'm sorry,' she moaned after a while. 'I don't mean to cry.'

'No, no,' he soothed. '*I'm* sorry. I'm sorry I was such a selfish bastard today. Leaving you all alone like that.'

'I knew you couldn't help it. I knew you had to go to work.'

His hold tightened on her, and his caresses developed a different sort of energy. Soon he was kissing her, tenderly, and then passionately, and she was clinging to him and giving him her all as if there were no tomorrow. Then before she knew it, to her thrilled excitement, he was hoisting her up in his arms and carrying her into his bedroom.

She was so glad he'd shaved.

# CHAPTER TWELVE

BREAKFAST was beautiful. After a night of passion, and long slow love as the dawn was breaking, Ariadne's husband chose to make her fresh orange juice and toast and bring it to her in bed. Then later, while he was showering, she cooked him some of the delicious little *bougatsas* with custard Thea often made for her uncle, and a nourishing spinach and feta omelette to sustain him in the workplace.

'Being married has its compensations,' Sebastian observed. As he smiled at her across the breakfast table, admiring her with his eyes in her shorts and pretty top, she allowed a wild, little hope to lift its head. What if they decided to play it for real? What if he asked her to stay?

When it was time for him to leave for work he kissed her long and deeply, though their lips were already bruised with kissing. 'I'd love to stay with you today,' he murmured. 'But I have some news for my employees that can't wait.'

'Is it about Thio's contract?' she guessed.

He nodded, scanning her face, and said carefully, 'It means quite a lot to Celestrial. There have been some worried faces in the office. I know you aren't comfortable with the circumstances, but the outcome has been very good for us. And...' he squeezed her hands '...let me know how it goes with the solicitor.'

After he'd gone and she'd cleared the breakfast dishes, she

found the firm of solicitors in the phone directory and booked an appointment. She had the option of Monday or Tuesday, but Monday seemed too close, so she opted for Tuesday. Fingers crossed there'd be something to inherit. Of course she was curious to know, but she couldn't suppress the thought that, once she had her inheritance in her possession, there was nothing to keep her here with Sebastian. It would be time for her to leave.

And go...where?

Sebastian drove into work whistling along to songs on the radio, preserving the buoyant, relaxed mood another night of passion had created by carefully controlling his thoughts. Some apprehension of having slid deeper into his glorious entanglement with Ariadne Giorgias lurked at one corner of his mind, but not to worry. He'd been moved by people before, and no doubt he would be again. The trick was not to get emotionally attached.

So she'd had a rift of some sort with her uncle and aunt. Families had conflicts, that was life, and there was no point letting a woman's distress play upon his heartstrings. An utterly impermissible notion had crept into his head while he'd been comforting her in the night, and he worried he might have said something reckless in the heat of the moment. She hadn't mentioned anything about it this morning, so perhaps he'd dreamed it. But there'd been a look in her eyes, a certain look he knew he must not encourage.

He doubted if *he* had that look. He'd never been a very emotional guy, despite what his family seemed to think.

Anyway, today was a day for celebration. He could hardly wait to assemble his employees and break the news.

A cheer went up at the meeting when he told them. If he'd been a different kind of boss they might have dared to pop a few champagne corks, but they restricted themselves to grinning, back-slapping and general loony happiness.

By mid-morning, it was clear not much work was likely to be

done this day. And with his own obsessive need to luxuriate in recollections of the night, he could hardly hold it against his workforce. He could have spent the day watching Celestrial's share price zoom on the stock market, but he kept wondering what Ariadne was doing. Cooking? He grinned to himself. That perky little vase filled with pretty leaves came back to him. He resisted as long as he could—it wouldn't be kind to give her any false ideas—but then he sprang up suddenly and grabbed his jacket.

'I'm leaving for the day,' he told a startled Jenny on his way out. 'Oh, and...hey, why don't you take the rest of the day off?'

He wasn't a romantic guy, by any means, but flowers should have a presence on other occasions too, not just funerals.

He stopped off at a couple of places on the way home. Searching for his wallet to pay the florist, he came upon Ariadne's passport in the inside pocket of his jacket. He patted it. At least he could definitely certify she was still in the country.

Agnes had phoned to say she didn't feel well enough to come in. Ariadne had the villa all to herself.

Feeling lethargic after her late night, she took Sebastian's laptop up to bed with her, propped herself up on some pillows, and composed a letter to her old university requesting a reissue of her degree certificates. Then she spent some time scrolling the ads on one of the major Sydney job network sites. Perhaps once she'd assembled her testimonials, she could find employment in Sydney. If she could find a flat not too far away, perhaps she and Sebastian would stay in touch. He might take her out some time, to dinner, or a movie. They might meet for coffee, or...

Her heart panged. What a fool she was. As if people who'd been lovers ever met for coffee.

Sounds from downstairs startled her, and before she could shelve the laptop she heard the familiar footsteps bounding up the stairs.

'Oh, there you are.' Sebastian's tall form appeared in the doorway and her heart leaped up in surprise when she saw he seemed to be laden with flowers and packages.

'What are you doing?' He deposited his armful on the floor and sprawled on the bed beside her.

'Job hunting. What are *you* doing?' She craned to see the flowers. Roses interspersed with white alyssum. 'Are they for me?'

'For the house.' His thick black lashes swept down and screened his gaze. 'It's such a shemozzle at work I've taken the day off. Here, let me see that.' He peered over her shoulder at the screen at the advertisement she'd been investigating. 'Ah. Have you done this sort of thing before?'

She nodded. 'In Athens. And I've done a bit of study and training in antiquities. I *could* work in a museum.'

'Well, you shouldn't have much trouble finding something you like. *I'd* give you a job. Like *that*.'

She smiled and raised her brows flirtily. 'What as?'

He kissed her neck. 'I'd think of something. That reminds me.' He glanced appreciatively around the room. 'I've been meaning to say, everything looks—fantastic. In fact, last night I could have sworn my mother had been here, though I don't think even she makes the *walls* sparkle. Agnes must have been inspired.'

She nodded without speaking, and he continued to hold her in his dark, smiling gaze. 'It wasn't Agnes, though, was it?'

'Some of it,' she said with a shrug. 'I just gave her a helping hand. She isn't very well, you know. Her asthma's pretty bad at the moment. It's a large villa for one elderly woman to clean on her own.'

'Yeah.' He frowned, and let out a sigh. 'I should have thought. I s'pose it's too much for her. I did notice she wasn't performing up to scratch.'

'You did?' She widened her eyes in mock astonishment.

He laughed and gave her a little shake. 'Yes, I *did*, but I didn't want to sack her. I think she relies on the money, and…well, you know, Esther was fond of her.'

There was a beat of silence. 'Esther. Your wife.'

He met her gaze, then lowered his thick, black lashes. 'Yeah.'

She screwed up her courage to say carefully, 'What happened with Esther? Did—she die?'

His face smoothed to become expressionless. 'Cancer. Three years ago.'

'Oh.' She had the sensation of walking on extremely fragile eggshells. 'That must have been—awful for you.'

'It was awful for *Esther*.'

'Oh, of course it was, of course.' She could see talking about it was painful for him, but wasn't sure how to back out of the topic gracefully. 'You—you must have suffered a lot too.'

He shot her a glance, then lowered his gaze and said harshly, 'I was absolutely fine. Esther was the one who suffered. I was the selfish bastard who survived.'

'Oh, oh.' Her heart clenched. She stared at him in distress, urgent to think of some soothing thing to alleviate the excruciating moment. In her desperation she risked touching him, and stroked his arms, relieved when he didn't draw away. 'Someone—someone has to survive to tell the story.' He didn't answer, and, still stroking him, she babbled on to fill the silence, 'The story of Esther, I mean. Who she was, and what she was like.'

She held her breath. Had she said the wrong thing?

He glanced up at her then with a shrug, and his grim expression relaxed. 'That's truer than you know. But let's not worry about it right now. See what I've brought you.'

He reached for the roses and put them in her arms, then piled a wide, slim black box on top.

'Oh, thank you. They're *heavenly*,' she breathed, inhaling their sweet heady fragrance. 'And wow. Not chocolates! *Wicked.*

Look at the size of this box. *Theos*, these are my downfall. How did you know?' She lay the roses down beside her and lifted the chocolates to smell the box.

He smiled, a sexy, sinful smile, his dark eyes flickering over her with a hungry, wolfish look. 'Well, I *am* a genius. You said so yourself.'

She laughed and he took her in his arms and kissed her, rolling her onto her back, oblivious of the gifts they were crushing in an embrace that grew hotter and steamier by the second. Desire flared in her again with an almost scary readiness as he undid the buttons on her top for an urgent and delicious exploration of her breasts.

The more she had of him, it seemed to her, hungrily releasing *his* shirt buttons, the more she had to have of him. After a long, writhing, mindless time she grew conscious of things sticking into her side, and broke from his arms, gasping in air.

'Oh, no,' she said when she could. 'The chocolates. They'll be crushed.'

He reached for the roses and lifted them to safety. The box wasn't too badly squashed, apart from the corners.

She examined it. 'I think it's only the box that's damaged.'

They surveyed each other, shirts hanging open, pleasure still tingling in her veins, desire shimmering in the air, unappeased.

She smiled. 'Hungry?'

His eyes gleamed. 'Not for chocolate.'

She flicked him a glance from beneath her lashes, then tore off the cellophane wrapper. 'Oh,' she sighed, opening the box and viewing the sumptuous array. She closed her eyes to inhale the intoxicating aroma. 'I'm so glad you've taken the day off.'

'The whole weekend. First time in—ages. Feel like doing a little sightseeing tomorrow?' He leaned forward and planted a sexy little kiss on her shoulder.

'Yeah! That'd be great.' She smiled, pretending to consider the chocolates, enjoying the play as he delayed the moment of pouncing on her with a little conversational chit-chat.

'What would you like to see?'

Aware of his fingers stroking a shivery path down her spine, she murmured hazily, 'The Katherine Gorge.'

His brows twitched. 'How about the Opera House?'

'Seen it.'

The chocolates looked a little on the soft side, but were silky and succulent notwithstanding. She bent her head to study the key to the varieties. 'Nougat, almond or strawberry liqueur?' She glanced up at him. 'What I'd really like, if you had the time, would be to see my parents' cottage.'

He was watching her with a sensual gleam in his eyes, but when she said that his brows lifted. 'Great. Do you know the address?'

She popped a cherry liqueur into her mouth, closing her eyes as its deliciousness melted on her tongue and mingled with her mouth juices. After a blissful second she said, 'Off by heart. It's in wobbly writing in all my old story books.'

'You've never been back since, have you?' A dark flame smouldered in his eyes.

'No. I've often longed to see it again. I'm quite excited.'

His lids were heavy and slumberous. 'Are you?' He ran his finger from her mouth to her shorts' zip and said huskily, 'Well, I'm *very* excited.'

She could see by the bulge in his groin that he wasn't exaggerating.

Excitement was infectious. It turned her voice to a throaty purr. 'Sure you won't join me in a little Cheri Suisse?'

'That's exactly what I intend.'

He bent and slipped his tongue into her mouth at the same time as his rough, urgent hands finished unbuttoning her top, and slid around her back to unfasten her bra.

She felt her blood ignite. A hot, sexy kiss mingled with chocolate was almost too much pleasure to endure at one time. While his clever tongue tickled her sensitive mouth, her hungry hands convulsively enjoyed the textures and contours of his bronzed chest and washboard-hard abdominals.

'Delicious,' he said after another steamy while, drawing away from her.

She bent to lick off a chocolatey smear she'd left on his right nipple, causing his skin to shiver and the flat little bead to perk up. 'Ooh,' she said, savouring the flavours of chocolate and raw salty man. 'Your nipple likes chocolate.'

'You're a little tease,' he rumbled, his voice a deep, sultry murmur. She made a move to take another chocolate but he swiftly grabbed her hand and held it still. 'My turn.' He reached for the box, and his long, tanned fingers hung poised over the selection. 'Ah. What else but raspberry?'

He held his selection between his palms for a second, his eyes gleaming wickedly. 'Now let's see what happens.'

In a rapid movement he smeared the chocolate over her breasts, then, with a laugh that was halfway a growl, bent to suck each of her nipples. She shivered with delight as lightning raced along her nerve endings, tightening the tingling points and igniting them with an explosive hunger.

Her shorts came off in the sexy tussle. When his marauding tongue and ruthless, ravaging hands had turned her blood to wildfire and she'd cried and moaned her pleasure, it became her turn again.

Perhaps she was running a fever, because in a surge of reckless daring she sat up and placed her hands on his belt buckle, and purred, 'Let's see what we have here.'

With hands that trembled at their own unaccustomed boldness, she released the button and eased down his zip. He watched her face, sensual amusement dancing in his aroused eyes like searing points of flame. He lifted his lean hips a little to assist her in dragging off the confining clothes, then kicked them away altogether.

'Oh, my goodness,' was her sincere reaction.

His erection sprang thick and proud and virile, swelling and pulsing before her wide eyes. She stared, not missing the full and violent impact of its message.

Daunted, almost unconsciously she licked her lips.

Politely, but with a wicked grin, Sebastian offered her the chocolate box. She blinked. In truth, for a cowardly instant she nearly blenched at the challenge.

But what was she? An inexperienced virgin, or a married woman able to give and receive pleasure in the privacy of her husband's bedroom? The bravest woman he'd ever met? With grave care she selected a couple of chocolate caramels, then, with a long glance at him from beneath her lashes, melted the rich creamy beauties between her hands.

It took her a while to come to terms with what she was about to try, so she held the smouldering guy in suspense for seconds, letting her eyes flicker to his rampant penis, rubbing her hands together while she slicked the gooey, sensuous chocolate over her palms.

Her playmate waited, immobile apart from the barely perceptible rise and fall of his bronzed chest, his black eyes glittering with fever, and the air in the room seemed to tauten to a dangerous pitch.

As she eyed his virile length a tiny, expectant drop of pure masculine essence pearled on the tip, and she felt her mouth water and her folds moisten in helpless excitement. Then, just before the tension reached flashpoint, she smeared her mouth voluptuously with chocolate, then gripped his rosy rod and held him tight, sliding her hands up and down the throbbing shaft.

Sebastian let out a small groan, and to her intense satisfaction she felt him swell and become even harder in her grasp. Sympathetically, her nipples, her breasts, her sweet tender place all swelled too and yearned with desire.

Shudders of pleasure roiled through Sebastian's big frame, and though he held himself quite still she noticed a seductive line of sweat appear on his upper lip. Not to be called a coward, she knelt down then and stroked his amazing length from base to velvet tip with her tongue, smoothing the chocolate off as she went.

She felt so unbelievably hot and sexy and reckless, she was revelling in her brave exploration of the situation, but at that point things escalated beyond her control.

As though all at once driven crazy by her ministrations to his throbbing rod, Sebastian suddenly grabbed her and flipped her onto her back. He scrabbled at the side of the bed for the condom packet, ripped one open with his teeth, then with swift hands rolled the sheath on.

For a suspenseful, exhilarating second the hungry, hard, rapidly breathing guy softly combed her curls with his lean, smooth fingers, his dark eyes devouring her chocolate-smeared nudity like molten fire while he magically tickled her already moist delta into a state of electric wildness.

Then with a possessive little growl he covered her with his gorgeous lean body and plunged himself into her willing flesh.

# CHAPTER THIRTEEN

ARIADNE cooked dinner that night and made Sebastian her kitchen-aide. She had no doubt he surprised himself with his ability to wash herbs, to peel, chop and dice to her rigorous standards, but she wasn't surprised. She'd had experience of the guy's artful fingers.

The preparation of dinner was really a pleasant extension of the bedroom and the subsequent bath, in which she'd learned so much more about giving and receiving. And the meal didn't suffer from the flirty camaraderie that had seemed to spring from their intimate adventures.

'There's something so sexy about watching a woman cook,' her husband said, kissing her neck as she stood at the sink.

'What's really sexy is a man *helping* a woman to cook,' she threw over her shoulder.

She'd decided on the simple, nourishing peasant food Thea believed every Greek husband thrived on, from the humble fisherman to the shipping magnate. When Sebastian had performed his part of the chopping, he perched on a kitchen stool and watched her toss some delicate calamari rings in the pan for their first course, in the absence of retsina sipping a glass of chilled white wine. She placed a little platter of nibbles at his elbow, plump olives and rice-stuffed dolmades that he dipped into a tzatziki she'd whipped up with some yoghurt, cucumber and lemon juice.

She could feel Sebastian's curious gaze appraising her in her pretty skirt and top, watching her reach for things, pause and check things, open the oven door to inspect the progress of the moussaka. He was still surprised, she guessed. He hadn't expected his mail-order bride to know her way around a kitchen. And he seemed warmly receptive to her ideas, including the one of hiring more staff to assist Agnes.

It gave her a surge of hope. He clearly enjoyed seeing his home glowing and comfortable and cared for. Perhaps he would start to see how lovely it could be to have a woman always here at the heart of things. Someone to keep the love fires burning.

On Saturday he drove her to her old street, as promised, but the cottage she dimly remembered from her early childhood had been replaced by an apartment block. Still, she took some photos of the street sign, and a tree she convinced herself had been there all along. Disappointed, she asked Sebastian if he would mind taking her to see the place where her parents were buried.

Something flickered in his eyes at her request, as though he felt taken aback, then he agreed readily enough. They took a little time to find the location on the Internet, then drove to Waverley, which she was surprised to see was very close to Bronte.

The modest headstones they sought were on a cliff, stalwart against the ocean breeze, if a little stained by the weather. Ariadne read the sad little inscriptions, shaken by the peaceful solemnity of the place, and laid some purple flowers at their base. Here were her roots, in *this* earth, this grass, this sacred ground.

When would she feel she belonged?

She saw Sebastian's watchful gaze flicker from her to her surroundings, and had the uncanny notion he'd read her mind.

He observed, 'Your father must have loved Australia to choose to be buried here.'

'He was dead,' she snapped. 'He had no choice.'

Shocked at her own terseness, she turned away, misting with tears all at once. How pathetic she was, grieving for a *place* when she was young, alive and had her health, while her parents' youthful lives had been so rudely interrupted.

She wiped her eyes, then felt a strong arm slip around her waist.

'He chose to live here,' Sebastian said firmly. 'He chose an Australian wife. He chose this as his child's homeland. *Your* homeland.'

'I *know* that, all right? I know.' She slipped from his grasp.

'Hey. Steady there.' He touched her bare arm, sliding his hand around the muscle as though unable to keep from savouring the texture of her flesh. He frowned. 'Isn't there anything in this country you like?'

He looked so mystified, with his dark eyes so serious and intent, his black brows bristling in puzzlement, her heart shook all at once with love for him.

She said softly, 'There is, lover. There's *you.*'

She stood up on tiptoe and kissed him on the lips, her hands on his ribs, relishing the charge of response in his lean, vibrant body as he held her hard against him and took command of the exchange.

The flare-up was smoothed away, and afterwards she couldn't remember why she'd been upset. She smiled wonderingly down at the graves.

'It's been good to see this place. I've often imagined it. Now I have, I don't really feel they're sad, you know, Sebastian? I think somehow they're up there in the ether, smiling and wafting around like clouds. Do you...?' She turned to look at him. 'Do you feel like that when you go to visit Esther's resting place?'

His eyes slid away from her, and he bit out rather curtly, 'I don't go.'

On the way back to the car, Sebastian held her hand, but he was silent on the way home. He'd withdrawn a little, and she couldn't help brooding. She'd told him she liked him, but despite his warmth he hadn't responded in kind. Had *like* been too close to that other word? The one she longed to hear?

That evening they drove up into the Blue Mountains for some star-gazing through a giant telescope belonging to a friend. They stayed overnight in a chalet, and the next day explored some of the little villages interspersed with the magnificent scenery, including some truly awe-inspiring gorges. But as the weekend drew to a close, though there'd been good times, she'd had anxious ones as well. Times when Sebastian was with her in the flesh, but was it only the flesh?

Could her instincts be so wrong? Did such a passionate, tender guy only feel desire?

On Monday evening, the day before she was due to receive her inheritance, he arrived home earlier than usual.

'Hello, beautiful,' he said, embracing her. 'Good day?' Though he smiled his dark eyes were searching, as if he had something on his mind.

As she served the meal they chatted about small things, the minor comings and goings of each others' days, but Ariadne was conscious of him being preoccupied.

Was it her imagination, or was he cooler than usual, though he praised her for the dinner? When the meal was over and she was about to put the tea on, he took her arm. 'Leave that. Come and sit down. I need to ask you something.'

His lean, dark face was serious, and she felt a stir of anxiety about what was coming, especially when he chose his armchair rather than the sofa next to her.

He dug into his jacket pocket, and produced an opaque plastic bag and handed it across. 'I picked this up this morning.'

He watched her so intently she hardly dared open it. Wonderingly, she shook out a slim parcel of tissue paper. As she unrolled the paper, with a flash of blue something cool and heavy slipped into her hand. She gasped to see her own bracelet of sapphires, their glittering fires as brilliant as ever.

'Oh.' Stunned, she stared at it for seconds, then looked quickly up at him. 'How? Where'd you get it?'

He reached into his jacket pocket again and fished out her passport holder. 'I found this in my pocket the other day. I'd forgotten all about it being in this suit. Today I took the passport out to flick through and the receipt for the pawnbroker slipped out. Then I remembered something the jeweller mentioned on our wedding day.' He made a sardonic grimace. 'Lucky you only hocked this. They ripped you off pretty disgracefully, I'd say.'

She flushed. 'I know they did. But there was no need for *you* to worry, Sebastian. At the time I just needed some—temporary funds. I always intended to redeem the bracelet myself. Once…'

'Once you had your inheritance.'

She blinked. 'Yes.'

He continued to scrutinise her face. Her heart started to thud and she felt a flush mount to her neck. 'Ariadne…'

He leaned forward in his chair, his dark eyes grave and compelling. 'I don't want to pry into your private affairs, but I need to understand. You said you weren't rich. But how so? How can a Giorgias be so short of cash she has to hock her jewellery?'

She tried to sidle out of explaining. 'Being a Giorgias doesn't mean I'm rich. This bracelet was a gift. An art gallery doesn't pay its employees massive salaries.'

'Even so…' He levelled his intent dark gaze at her, and pinned her to the point. 'You flew out here to meet me, you rejected me at first, then you were keen to get married the very next day. What was suddenly so urgent?' His intelligent dark eyes scoured her face in an uncompromising probe. 'It's time for the truth, my sweet.'

The implication stung, and she stiffened. 'What do you mean, "it's time for the *truth*"? I've never lied to you.'

'Well…you have to admit you weren't exactly open about your reasons.'

She could feel the walls closing in, and when she didn't answer, he said quietly, 'It's to do with your uncle and aunt, isn't it?'

She gave a shrug of admission. 'I suppose.'

'If you were short of funds, though, *why*…why couldn't you apply to them to bail you out?'

Her flush deepened as she felt herself twisting on the spit. 'I have told you most of it already.' She braced for deep humiliation. 'This is hard for me, Sebastian. Are you sure you want to…?'

His gaze was firm and unequivocal and capitulated. 'All right. It's true that I flew here for a holiday. At least, that was what I *thought* I was doing.' She saw his eyes flick to her suddenly shaking hands. 'I—I just couldn't bear to tell you the worst part. I feel so—embarrassed.' Her voice croaked in her throat, but she forced herself to expose her humiliation with as much dignity as she could muster. 'It was Thio who booked my holiday. It was supposed to be a gift. I didn't understand his real intention until I was on the plane.'

He frowned. 'His *real* intention. You mean, that you were coming to meet your prospective bridegroom?'

She lifted her shoulders in wry bitterness. 'I didn't know I had one. They mentioned I'd be meeting the Nikosto family. I didn't realise my uncle had struck a deal with *you* until something he said when I was getting on the plane. So I phoned him from the plane. That's when I—found out.'

There was a stunned flicker in his eyes. 'My God.'

She nodded. 'You see? When I arrived here I discovered nothing had been paid for. I had some money of my own, of course, to pay for meals and taxis, that sort of thing, but the big costs, the hotel and the tours, had never been paid.'

'And then you met me,' he said grimly. 'And the trap was complete.' He said in a constrained voice, 'And I—wasn't very kind to you at all.'

She shot him a low glance. 'Perhaps not,' she said, and saw him wince.

She spread her hands. 'I have to admit I panicked. In a strange country, with hardly any real money, I didn't have many choices. And it seemed clear to me…' She met his appalled gaze, then cast down her lashes. 'You didn't want to marry me, anyway. Not really, but you were just prepared to grit your teeth and go through with it for the sake of your company.'

He compressed his chiselled mouth into a straight, grim line, then nodded. 'I admit it. Your uncle—had made me very angry.'

She nodded, clasping her hands, her heart aching with mortification and pained love for her uncle and aunt. 'When I rang Thea to find out what had gone wrong, she said…' her voice wobbled '…you *needed* to marry me.'

'Oh, hell.' He sprang across to the sofa and grasped her arms. 'Why didn't you tell me any of this?'

'Oh, well.' Her throat thickened, emotion rendering her voice gravelly. 'Try to understand. They're my *family*. I didn't want you to think badly of them. Thio doesn't mean to hurt, truly. They're old, you know. And they—they do love me. They do.' Tears washed into her eyes.

Sebastian looked sharply at her, comprehension and compassion colouring his eyes, then they veiled almost at once and he shook his head, frowning. A muscle twitched in his lean cheek.

She fought for control. 'I know what you're thinking, but they still cling to so many of the traditions, you see. Thio has always had so much power he thinks he can do as he likes. He just bulldozes over people, and Thea lets him get away with it.' She dashed a tear away with the back of her hand. 'After the scandal he thought he had to rescue my honour. He probably thought by forcing me into marriage with some eligible guy, as far away as possible, he was doing the very best thing for me.' She realised how that must have sounded, and quickly touched his hand. 'It's only by the greatest good luck the guy turned out to be *you*. It hasn't been such a bad thing after all, has it?'

With a thud in his chest Sebastian heard the note in her voice. Her tentative blue gaze, so warm and shyly questioning, pierced straight through his steel-plated resistance and touched some yearning part of him with a dangerous potency. God, but she was sweet. Everything a man could dream of in a woman, surely. For an instant he was intensely tempted to lower his guard, drag her into his arms and hold her vibrant lusciousness to him. But with a roaring pressure in his temples visions of Esther and all the nightmare days and nights crowded in on him, reminding him of how it could turn out.

There was no way he could risk it. Never again.

Luckily, adrenaline lent him the necessary iron to deal with the situation before it got out of control.

'No, not at all it hasn't,' he replied without blinking, 'but when did you say you were seeing that lawyer?'

'Tomorrow.'

'Good.'

Ariadne searched his cool resolute gaze and the blood drained from her heart. 'Oh.' Her smile was so tight it hurt. She stood up and stuttered, 'I—I s-suppose you've been thinking I've over-stayed my welcome.'

He lowered his lashes. 'No, no, not at all, but...' He hesitated, then chose his words with great care. 'It's been—fantastic having you here, but you need to have your money and your freedom of choice. Then you can decide what you want to do, and who with.'

She swallowed, half comprehending that the ground was sliding away from her. Desperation tempted her to say things her instincts were clanging alarm bells against. 'But what if I say now that I'd like to stay with *you*? What if I tell you that I…I'm in love with you?'

He closed his eyes then stepped backwards, increasing the distance between them. 'No, please… *Don't…*' He held up his hand as if to ward something off, and drew a deep breath. 'Look, Ariadne, it's better if we don't try to complicate what's been a fantastic time. We were both forced into this, and…I guess, we've naturally—bonded—to some extent.'

She opened her mouth to speak but he held up his lean hand again.

'No, we need to be realistic. Sweetheart, I'm very conscious I've been your first—lover.' A dark stain spread across his cheek-bones. 'People—people often think they've fallen in love with their first. It's all new, and it seems…' he made a jerky gesture '…*special* somehow. You know, you start seeing the world through rose-coloured glasses. Everything starts to look hopeful again. You can't wait to get home and see the person every day. You think about them all the time. *Worry* about them, all their little… But it can't last.'

The blood thundering in her ears made her head swim. Lighting on the one thing coming through loud and clear, she said, a treacherous tremor in her voice, 'You—don't want me, then?'

His dark face twisted and he turned his eyes away from her. 'Ariadne, think of this. Soon you'll have your money and your freedom of choice. And you'll look back on this inter-lude and think how lucky you were to escape from such a selfish bastard as Sebastian Nikosto.' He smiled, but it was more like a grimace.

Her heart ached so cruelly she could scarcely breathe but, gathering the last thin remains of her dignity about her, she croaked, 'I guess you'd prefer it if I left tomorrow.'

'No. *Hell*, no. Take as long as you need to find a job, and get settled. I'm very conscious of owing you a debt of gratitude for all you've done here. But, you know, *this*—' he waved his hand, and looked ruefully at her '—*us*, the way we started, it's been lovely, you're a gorgeous girl, but whatever it is we think we have between us is built on sand. Sooner or later you'll end up leaving anyway.' His voice rasped. 'Everybody does.'

# CHAPTER FOURTEEN

SEBASTIAN stared out at the rain squall sweeping across the harbour and wondered if Ariadne had reached her appointment without getting soaked. Things had been strained after their discussion, but when he'd offered to leave work to come home and drive her this morning, she'd asserted politely that she could get there under her own steam.

He'd felt gutted when he saw her morning face. Since last night he'd had a jagged feeling in his chest, as if he'd kicked something fragile, or done something very stupid.

In fact, she'd slept in the other room. He still felt raw when he thought of the savage night he'd endured, but, in truth, in some ways he'd been relieved. At least he hadn't taken advantage of her last night as well.

A concept was lurking on the edges of his mind, something so simple, so bright and elegant. If only he could grasp it firmly.

The afternoon in the office seemed interminable, and on a sudden what-the-hell impulse he grabbed his car keys and headed for the door.

On the way home he tried to think of some things he could say to reduce her hurt. The trouble was, he was a blundering fool where women were concerned. Take Esther…

In a strange coincidence, he'd nearly reached the turn-off to Waverley. For some reason, on an absolutely unprecedented impulse he took it, and drove slowly along the street until he found the entrance where he knew Esther's ashes had been slotted into a wall, along with those of thousands of other souls. He got out of the car and stood a while, perhaps an hour, wondering if he was facing some crazy sort of widower's crisis, then walked along the avenues, hunched against the rain, until he came to the one he'd visited that one time before.

There was a little brass plaque set in the wall with Esther's name on it. He stared at it for an age, trying to sense if Esther was present, remembering what Ariadne had said about her parents. He wiped the raindrops off the plaque with his sleeve, then took out his handkerchief and gave it a firmer polish.

The truth was, Esther wasn't there. Not that he could sense. She wasn't anywhere any more, except perhaps up there in the ether, smiling with the other clouds. He saw it then, the simple dazzling truth.

Ariadne was here and now, warm and alive and smelling of flowers. Seized with a buoyant burst of energy and purpose he sprinted to the car, his feet squelching in his wet shoes.

'You're a very rich woman,' the attorney said, his rainwater eyes and thinning grey hair in perfect harmony with his grey suit, pearl silk tie and dim, grey humour. 'Didn't your uncle ever inform you of your father's stake in Giorgias Shipping?'

Ariadne shook her head.

'Your dad inherited his small stake from his grandmother, while your uncle inherited his larger one from his father. Lucky for you, Giorgias Shipping has gone from strength to strength.' He smiled a watery smile. 'There's nothing stopping you from doing whatever you wish with your life, Mrs Nikosto. You can buy the Harbour Bridge if you like. Travel anywhere in the world.'

Anywhere except Naxos.

'Thank you.' Ariadne pasted on a smile, just as though she

weren't a creature composed almost solely of pain. She gathered her handbag, then rose and shook hands with the lawyer. As she made the descent in the lift, then walked free and rich into the Sydney rain, she realised she didn't want to go to Naxos anyway. There was no one for her there now.

Or anywhere.

Still, she had choices. Billions of them, it seemed, all of them empty. What did a woman do when her husband couldn't accept her love? She probably should find a taxi to take her home in time to cook his dinner. Instead, she turned listlessly in the direction of a travel agent she'd noticed in the Pitt Street Mall.


Sebastian closed the door behind him and tossed his keys on the hall table. He paused, listening. The house seemed curiously quiet. He strolled through the house and into the kitchen. Everything was neat and orderly, clean and pristine, but there was no aromatic pot simmering on the range. He opened the oven door.

Nothing.

No crisp salad waiting on the bench top. No cooking. No wife. Could she be sleeping?

With a sudden dread he bounded up the stairs two at a time, calling, 'Ariadne.'

In every direction emptiness met his gaze. No trace of her in his bedroom, or in the other room she'd taken to sleeping in since the fateful discussion. Her wardrobe was bare. No bottles on the vanity. No combs or brushes on her dressing table. His house, his life, back to a threadbare shell.

A single silky scarf hung from her doorknob, drifting softly on the breeze. Something about its soft fragility devastated him. He snatched it up and held it to his face to inhale the last trace of her perfume. With a tearing pain in his chest he tried to come to terms with the possibility the worst had happened. She'd left him.

Although where would she go?

It was too late to call the lawyer at work, so he phoned the guy at his home. No luck there. The man couldn't say where his beautiful wife had gone after he'd handed her the keys to her inheritance.

His bed had never felt so desolate. He was still awake when the dawn broke. A little after six, haggard and unshaven, he hastened for the front door at the sound of the bell. Ariadne? The silly little hope rose in his heart. Maybe she'd forgotten her key, been held up somehow and stayed in a hotel.

He opened the door and stared. Two elderly Greeks were on the porch, issuing a stream of conflicting instructions to a chauffeur who was unloading suitcases from a long black limousine. The Greek man was portly and moustachioed, his wife formally and expensively dressed for so early in the day, her warm pleasant face creased in anxiety.

'Careful with that, you fool,' the man blustered. 'No, no, not there, idiot. *There.*'

'Just a moment, Peri. *I'll* handle this. Bring the black one first, will you, my dear young man? I'll need that first. Then find the brown one with the pinstripe. Ah, excellent. Thank you, thank you.'

The elderly man turned. When he saw Sebastian his eyes widened, and at once he threw out his hands. 'Ah, my boy, my blessed, blessed *boy.*' He seized Sebastian with enthusiasm and kissed him on both cheeks. 'It's me. Peri. Your uncle, and you must call me Thio. And this is your Aunt Eleni.' He beamed and rubbed his hands. 'Where is my girl? Where's our Ariadne?'

As Sebastian dredged up the bald words and delivered his tidings, it was the wife who broke the ensuing silence. 'What? Are you saying she isn't *here*? Where, then?' There was a note of panic in her voice. 'Where in the world is she? What have you done with my *toula*?'

# CHAPTER FIFTEEN

ARIADNE adjusted her beach bag to cushion her back, and leaned on her elbows to watch the early morning surfers. Far out beyond the first line of breakers, a lone swimmer powered through the water in a leisurely freestyle, barely raising a splash. For a minute she watched, envying that assured, lazy crawl.

How she wished she could do it. It reminded her of a precious morning spent watching Sebastian in the surf on Bronte Beach. Though that was history now, just a bright, fleeting moment in time. Still, she'd done the right thing in leaving. She knew that with a deep certainty. If they'd gone on as they were, without a commitment of love on both sides, they'd have ended in tears sooner or later.

Better for it to be sooner, before her love had grown too deep for her to have the strength. The well of emotion connected to thoughts of her brief, disastrous marriage threatened to overflow again, and she was obliged to lift the corner of her tee shirt and dab at her eyes. She'd really have to stop giving way to this grieving soon. It was time to straighten her shoulders and do something worthwhile with her life.

Perhaps this place might help, with its echoes of that magic time in her childhood. Beaches might have been much the same the world over, but Noosa had a charm all its own. Perhaps it was the bush-scented air. She inhaled an aromatic whiff of it.

Tea tree, casuarina and eucalypt, mingled with salty sea. A unique blend of wild things. Or it might have been the emerald and turquoise waters, or the smooth black waterstones lining the pretty shores.

Sebastian was doing brilliantly, she'd read in the papers. Celestrial's share value had rocketed on the Stock Exchange. Thio would be impressed.

Sebastian wasn't the only one who'd racked up achievements. She'd travelled quite a lot of her homeland in the recent months, though there was still much left to see. She'd jolted along red-dirt outback tracks in a four-wheel drive, and slept by a campfire beneath the southern cross. She'd kayaked along the river of a red desert gorge carved out in primeval times, and swum in the pure, crystalline waters of a bottomless lake.

She'd slept in sleeping bags, buses, on hard dry ground and in hostels pared down to offer none but the most basic of human amenities. All of it had been rare and beautiful and exciting. She'd plunged into every adventure with all her heart, what was left of the battered thing, though the beauties she'd seen had been blurred often by tears and her yearning for the wonderful man who'd taught her how to love then at the last minute rejected her.

Now she was waiting. She'd done some research and found that her great-auntie Maeve was still a resident of Noosa, though currently away visiting relatives in Tasmania. Every time Ariadne thought of that her toes clenched in pleasure.

Relatives in Tasmania. Chances were, they were her relatives too.

The swimmer who'd been far out beyond the breakers had changed tack and was heading in now. He disappeared in a trough, then his dark head bobbed up and she saw him pause and look around, waiting. He caught the next wave with effortless ease, riding it in like a dolphin. Every flash of his powerful arms suggested he was lean and deeply tanned.

He vanished again for a couple of minutes. Next time she spotted him he was much closer to shore.

She narrowed her eyes behind her dark glasses. He was nearly level now with the braver surfers, the ones who weren't afraid of swimming out of their depths. Soon he'd be able to stand. His hair looked black, as black as Sebastian's, though from this distance the water darkened everyone's hair.

He body-surfed the next wave in and she saw him stand suddenly, steadying himself against the swell with his arms. He started to make his way in. She leaned forward, and her heart started a wild hammering.

She pushed up her sunglasses for a clearer look. The man was tall and beautifully proportioned, like an athlete. He was wide at the shoulders, narrow at waist and hips, and she could make out more of his features.

For heaven's sake, she *must* be insane. Incredible, but the further he advanced, the more he looked like Sebastian.

Her painfully thundering pulse thought it was true, but it couldn't be. She must be imagining things. Sebastian was in Sydney managing Celestrial, not rising from the sea before her like Poseidon. As she stared, frozen, other sights, sounds, everything else faded from her consciousness. All she was aware of was her lean, hard, beautiful husband, striding from the shallows and onto the beach, dripping, his gaze focused ahead.

A small silence fell around her. With a sense of unreality, Ariadne turned to watch him walk past her and continue on a further thirty metres to the rinse-off shower at the edge of the beach.

Apparently unaware of her presence, he rinsed his hair and smoothed his hands over his virile chest and arms. Arms that had once been hers. Then he turned off the shower and strolled a little way to a small heap on the sand, muscles rippling in his long back and powerful thighs as he stooped to pick up a towel.

Ariadne's heart made a savage thud. Hadn't he noticed her?

She couldn't imagine he wouldn't have, when he stood out to her in any crowd. In fact she was forever seeing him in impossible places. And why was he in Noosa? He never took holidays. A horrible thought struck her. Could he be here with someone? Someone *new*?

She could hardly expect him to feel kindly towards her, but if he walked away without acknowledging her she'd die. She sat up straight and still, eyes closed, hardly daring to hope, her tremulous heart on a precipice, her nerves as tense as wires.

A shadow fell between her and the sun and she opened her eyes, to be momentarily dazzled. 'Ariadne.' When she adjusted to the light she looked up to meet her husband's dark intent gaze.

Every instinct in her being rushed heart and soul to welcome him, but she fought back the impulse to leap up and throw herself into his arms.

'Hello, Sebastian.'

He hesitated a second, then dropped down beside her on the sand. As he leaned to kiss her cheek his familiar masculine aura swamped her and the old sexual connection impacted on her with massive, weakening force.

She closed her eyes and said faintly, 'What—what are you doing here?'

'Passing through. How about you?'

As he examined her sunlight caught the gleams in his dark eyes. He was dressed now in shorts and a loose white tee shirt that enhanced his tan. Drops of water sparkled on his brows and lashes. Perhaps she imagined it, but he seemed thinner. Even his face appeared leaner, the lines around his mouth more deeply etched.

'Me too. I'm just here—temporarily.'

'Oh.'

She cast down her lashes. 'I've been—doing a bit of travelling around Australia. Reconnecting with my birthplace. Thought

I'd stay here in Queensland a while, since winter's just around the corner.'

There was a strained silence. He broke it first, nodding. 'Right. Good. Well, you've always wanted to see the country. So tell me. Is it up to your expectations?'

Thinking of the places she'd visited, her heart swelled with inexpressible emotion. 'Oh-h-h. *Better*. Better than I could ever describe in a million years. It's stunning. Spectacular. Who'd ever think a desert would be so beautiful? And the people. Everyone here is so kind and friendly and warm.'

'Warmer than the Greeks?'

'No.' She gave a shaky laugh. 'Not warmer than the Greeks. No one is warmer than Greeks.'

There was another silence, then he said lightly, 'I guess I thought that since you're a rich woman now you might have chosen to wing your way back to Naxos.' He looked keenly at her.

She met his narrowed gaze. 'No. My long-term plans are for here.'

His brows shot up. *'Here?'*

'No, no, not Noosa. Sydney, I think.'

His eyes lit, then veiled almost at once. 'Sydney? Oh. Good.' He nodded. 'That'll be—great.'

His black brows drew together. The air thundered with vibrations. She was dying to ask what he was really doing in Noosa, but she was too afraid of the answer to risk it.

The silence grew thick with unaskable questions, and this time it was she who broke it. 'I see that Celestrial is doing very well. I read all about you in the paper. They're calling you a whizz-kid. Congratulations. You must be celebrating.'

He gave a shrug. 'Thanks, but—' he glanced at her '—since I lost you, nothing seems worth celebrating.'

Emotion welled in her throat. 'Oh. I—suppose we lost each other.' Her voice was so husky it could have been shovelled up.

He stared down at the sand, then looked at her with an intent, serious glance. 'Look, would you consider coming up to the hotel and having breakfast with me? There are some things I need to say to you.'

Her heart thrilled with an anticipation so intense it was hard to determine whether it felt like joy or anguish. Still, she had to protect herself. Had to beware of his capacity to hurt her. What if it was the divorce he wanted to discuss?

'Breakfast sounds good,' she said. 'Where—are you staying?'

'The Sheraton.'

'Yeah? That's a coincidence. That's where I'm holed up.' She looked sharply at him, then said, all at once out of breath, '*Is* it a coincidence, Sebastian?'

He hesitated. 'Not exactly.'

He stood up and held out his hand. Nervous of touching him with her senses already haywire, she disregarded the offer of assistance and scrambled up herself. The quick movement made her slightly giddy, and she swayed a bit.

His hand snaked out to grasp her arm and steady her. 'Careful.'

Predictably, his fingers left a ring of the dangerous old fire burning on her arm like a brand.

As they strolled along Hastings Street, under the poinciana trees, past all the tourists breakfasting in the sidewalk cafés and thronging the gelaterias, she babbled on about her travels, wondering what it was he had to say to her, her brain in a haze, though her body seemed to be so sharply, vibrantly attuned to every part of him. Was it actual months since they'd been lovers?

He hardly said much, just kept nodding and gazing at her as if he couldn't look away, drinking her in from head to toe in her tee and shorts and sandals, his eyes glittering as they did when he was in the grip of strong emotion.

'You have a tan,' he observed at one point, his voice deep and gravelly.

She nodded.

His eyes flickered over her. 'You look—more beautiful than ever.' He shoved his hands in his pockets. 'Sort of glowing. So—what are your long-term plans?'

They'd paused in front of the lifts at the Sheraton.

After a second's hesitation, she said, 'Well, I've decided what I want to do in Australia. I'm thinking of building shelters for homeless people.' His brows shot up and she added quickly, 'Oh, I know Sydney already has shelters, but I want to make my own contribution. I can easily afford it. I'll start with one. Find some good people to work it so I can learn the ropes of running a charity.' She met his gaze fleetingly. 'Well, you know, it's terrifying not knowing where you're going to sleep the next night.' Her chin wobbled. 'I'll never forget how that felt.'

'I know,' he said, his eyes flooding with warmth and remorse. 'Of course you won't.' He clenched his jaw, and turned sharply away from her. After a moment he added, 'That's—that's a wonderful idea, I think. You'll—you'll do it very well.'

'I hope so,' she mumbled, her throat so tight her voice was a croak. 'I know I'm pretty green. I have a lot to learn.'

He grimaced. 'Don't we all?'

In the lift, their close proximity became quite agonising, with all the unspoken emotion fogging up the airwaves. She wished she could talk to him properly, open up her heart and voice the real things between them. Instead she said, her voice wobbling with the effort of sounding calm, 'Did you know, Sebastian, that Fraser Island is made entirely of *sand*? And there's a lake there, so deep no one has ever plumbed the bottom, but its water is as clear and fresh and pure as a mountain spring. Held there absolutely by sand. Did you know that?'

He stared at her, his eyes so dark they were black, then with a little groan he grabbed her and dragged her against him.

He held her against his lean, hard body for a long glorious time, stroking her hair, his bristly morning jaw grazing her forehead. Tears of loss for the love they might have had welled up from the bottomless spring in her heart, and she had a good weep against his chest. She could feel his big, strong heart beating against her cheek.

At last, after soaking up the strength of his healing essence for a while, she noticed that the lift doors had opened and people were outside, gawking in.

'Oops,' Sebastian rasped. 'Our floor.'

Sebastian's suite was much like hers, she noticed through her misty haze. Opulent. Enormous bedroom, plush sofas, views across the sea to heaven, and a delightful balcony where breakfast could be set, if there was a point when one was eating alone. Clothes were spilling out of his suitcase, and he had the bedroom in a bit of a shambles already.

Recovering from her shameful excess of lift emotion, she said brightly, 'How—how did you know I was here?'

'I remembered you told me once about your parents bringing you here for a holiday. I thought it was worth a try. I'd tried everywhere else I could think of.'

'Did you?' She dropped her gaze and mumbled, 'I should have left a note, I suppose. It was a—a spur-of-the-minute thing. You know, I just—just…'

'I know.' A flush darkened his tan. 'I hurt you.'

There was nothing she could say to express how much, so she just looked away, pained at the memories.

He said fiercely, his voice rough and deep, 'I'm so sorry. I think when I met you I got—caught up in a tangle over my first wife. I guess you could say I had guilt about falling in love again. You know, unresolved grief, or whatever it is they call it.'

*Falling in love again.* Had he, though?

'You know, when I met you, I was—overwhelmed.' His voice grew deep and gruff and thick. 'I couldn't believe my luck when you asked me to marry you that day. And at *once*. God, I was euphoric. I'd have done anything to have you. *Anything.*'

Her stomach clenched and she said in a low voice, well, it was wonderful of you to take me on. I was so very grateful.'

'I guess.' The strong lines of his face tautened. 'Though if I'd had any *idea*… It was clear you were worried about money, but if I'd known the full extent of just how desperate you *were* that day…' His jaw clenched, and he said fiercely, 'I'd have found some way to…' He punched a fist into his palm, and the muscles bunched in his bronzed arms. 'That old devil. I still feel as if I've let him off the hook too lightly. But only because of Eleni.'

'Eleni?' She looked quickly at him. 'Do you mean *Thea*?'

He nodded. 'Thea, yes. And, oh…' He flicked his forehead in sudden remembrance. 'Yeah, that's right, that's what I had to tell you. They're here.'

She started away from him and her eyes sprang wide. She glanced involuntarily about her as if her uncle and aunt might suddenly pop out of the furniture. '*Here*? In *Noosa*?'

'No, no, not *here*, thank God.' He pulled himself up at once. 'Oh, sorry. I know they're your family.' He looked apologetic, though his eyes glinted with sudden amusement. 'They're in Sydney. They stayed at our place for a few days until Agnes got sick of them, so they moved to a hotel. They must have flown out from Athens almost as soon as they heard we were married.'

'*What?*'

Her legs suddenly turned to jelly and she was forced to plump down on the bed. 'You mean, they've been here all this time?'

He sat down beside her, and slipped his arm around her. 'Indeed they have. They've been worried sick. Peri's hired every private detective on the eastern seaboard, and your aunt is nearly beside herself. She says she blames herself for your engagement to that rich guy in Greece.'

'Really?' She gave a sardonic shrug. 'Well, there's a turnaround. After the way they complained I was difficult. You're too spoilt, they said. On one occasion Thio actually accused me of being a *princess.*'

Even recalling the insult could still make her burn with indignation.

Something flickered in Sebastian's eyes, then he frowned and shook his head. 'He said *that*? Tsk.' He patted her shoulder sympathetically. 'I *think* they said there's been some sort of scandal about the guy since the wedding.' He narrowed his eyes in vague recollection. 'Oh, yeah, that's right. He came out.'

She gasped in incredulity. With the shocks coming so thick and fast, could she be hearing right? 'Are you sure?' she screeched. '*Demetri*? You mean he's gay?'

'Yep.' He nodded, frowning. 'I think that's what it was. You've been totally vindicated for defending yourself, Peri says.' He smiled. 'In fact in Greece you're practically a national hero.'

She stared at him in astonishment, then held her face in her hands and rocked backwards and forwards. '*Oh*. Oh, look, I just can't *believe* this. Demetri *gay*? So why did he want to marry me? Oh, you've no idea how the press bashed me over that. I went through an absolute *purgatory*.'

'Oh, well,' he said soothingly. 'That's all over now. I guess the guy had his reasons. The press are saying now that you've been given a raw deal. And you know, your aunt really had no idea your uncle had played that trick on you with the finances until you rang her. She's been giving him hell over it.' He dropped his gaze, grimacing. 'Especially since you married *me* and I wrecked your life.'

She gave him a quick look. 'Is that what she said?'

'Something like that.' His lashes flicked down and he looked embarrassed. 'Yeah, well... There's been some fairly heated family discussions, as you might imagine. Your aunt can be quite a formidable woman. At one point I actually came close to feeling sorry for old Peri. I shudder to think what it must be like in their suite at the Hyatt.'

It occurred to her that some of their old camaraderie was back. She beamed at him, so overjoyed to be actually sitting there with him again in the flesh, hope frothing in her heart like the eternal Aegean.

'I hope she *is* giving him a hard time. Still, I'm not sure I can face seeing them for a very long time.' She lifted her shoulders. 'You know, I thought they sent me out here to get rid of me. I don't think I can ever forgive them.'

'No one would blame you if you didn't.' He gazed down at her with tender concern. With a gentle movement, he stroked her cheek with lean fingers. 'But I don't honestly think that *was* ever their intention. They've been breaking their hearts over you.' He hesitated, then said softly, 'Almost as much as I have.'

'Oh.' Her heart caught with a tremulous hope and she drew a long shivery breath. 'Have you?'

He blinked, and the lines of his face tensed. 'I've been in hell.'

*Theos* forgive her, she didn't ever want to see Sebastian suffer, but it was good to hear that he'd cared when she'd suffered so much pain.

His lean, handsome face from cheekbone to jaw was set hard. 'I'm hoping—you can forgive *me*. I know you're enjoying your freedom. You've got the world on a string now. You can do whatever you like with your life.' He met her gaze, his dark eyes serious with sincerity and warmth. 'I'll do my best to tell you now without making a mess of it.' He hesitated, searching her face for reassurance, and she nodded encouragingly, hardly daring to breathe. 'I realised the truth the day you left. I rushed home to tell you, but like a fool I was too late.' He made a rueful grimace. 'Whatever you choose, the truth is, I love you, Ariadne. I can't pretend I don't want you to come back home and be my wife.'

She was moved to her soul. Her entire being filled with such thrilled, joyful relief she reached out to stroke his beloved face with both hands. 'Oh, Sebastian.'

'Do you—think you could love me?' His voice was as deep as a well, and though his eyes were uncertain his fingers strayed to her neck, and stroked the tender spot in her nape with a rock-solid surety she recognised. The sensation was so delicious it required an effort to talk. 'Even after the way I hurt you?'

'Yes, I do,' she breathed, thrilling all down her spine. 'I love you. I love you like mad.'

He closed his eyes. 'Thank God.' Then he kissed her long and deep.

She moulded herself to his familiar frame and surrendered herself to the rapturous mingling of love and mutual belonging. By the time she surfaced again she was giddy, from happiness as much as the lack of oxygen.

It didn't look as if breakfast was about to happen any time soon. Once started on a certain divine course, in typical fashion, Sebastian wasn't anxious to stop.

He sprawled on the bed and pulled her to him, murmuring, 'Why don't we start our honeymoon straight away?' He kissed her throat. 'We could go to Fraser Island if you like.'

'Oh, I'd *love* to go there with you.'

He adjusted his big lean frame so that they were each lying on their sides, heads supported on their elbows, face to face, chest to chest, hands to seeking hands. 'And afterwards, we could, if you liked, have a proper wedding in a church. But only if you want that, my darling. With the music and flowers, and all the families and everyone. Then if you want to we could visit Naxos. Make a grand triumphal tour.' With a thoughtful gleam in his eye he added, 'Lure your aunt and uncle back home.'

*My darling*, he'd called her. She imagined it all, being loved and accepted by Sebastian's family as a proper bride, not a bartered woman with no autonomy or equality. Mrs Nikosto. Mr and Mrs Nikosto. Her husband. Her proud, darling husband.

The words sang in her ears like music.

'What do you think?'

'I think yes, my darling Sebastian. Yes, and yes, and *yes*.' Unable to help herself, she punctuated each yes with a fervent little kiss.

Somehow then she found herself lying on her back, being kissed in every little nook and cranny by the lips she most desired in the world.

Sebastian ran out of things to say very soon, but she had no doubts about his enthusiasm. He expressed his feelings in other ways, convincing her of his wholehearted sincerity with the most passionate and ardent means at his disposal, to her intense and delightfully long-lasting pleasure.

# LARGER-PRINT BOOKS!

HARLEQUIN *Presents*

PASSION
GUARANTEED
SEDUCTION

## GET 2 FREE LARGER-PRINT
## NOVELS PLUS 2 FREE GIFTS!

**YES!** Please send me 2 FREE LARGER-PRINT Harlequin Presents® novels and my 2 FREE gifts (gifts are worth about $10). After receiving them, if I don't wish to receive any more books, I can return the shipping statement marked "cancel." If I don't cancel, I will receive 6 brand-new novels every month and be billed just $4.55 per book in the U.S. or $5.24 per book in Canada. That's a saving of at least 13% off the cover price! It's quite a bargain! Shipping and handling is just 50¢ per book.* I understand that accepting the 2 free books and gifts places me under no obligation to buy anything. I can always return a shipment and cancel at any time. Even if I never buy another book, the two free books and gifts are mine to keep forever.

176/376 HDN E5NG

| | |
|---|---|
| Name | (PLEASE PRINT) |

| | |
|---|---|
| Address | Apt. # |

| | | |
|---|---|---|
| City | State/Prov. | Zip/Postal Code |

Signature (if under 18, a parent or guardian must sign)

### Mail to the **Harlequin Reader Service:**
**IN U.S.A.:** P.O. Box 1867, Buffalo, NY 14240-1867
**IN CANADA:** P.O. Box 609, Fort Erie, Ontario  L2A 5X3

Not valid for current subscribers to Harlequin Presents Larger-Print books.

### Are you a subscriber to Harlequin Presents books
### and want to receive the larger-print edition?
### Call 1-800-873-8635 today!

\* Terms and prices subject to change without notice. Prices do not include applicable taxes. Sales tax applicable in N.Y. Canadian residents will be charged applicable provincial taxes and GST. Offer not valid in Quebec. This offer is limited to one order per household. All orders subject to approval. Credit or debit balances in a customer's account(s) may be offset by any other outstanding balance owed by or to the customer. Please allow 4 to 6 weeks for delivery. Offer available while quantities last.

**Your Privacy:** Harlequin Books is committed to protecting your privacy. Our Privacy Policy is available online at www.eHarlequin.com or upon request from the Reader Service. From time to time we make our lists of customers available to reputable third parties who may have a product or service of interest to you. If you would prefer we not share your name and address, please check here. ☐

**Help us get it right**—We strive for accurate, respectful and relevant communications. To clarify or modify your communication preferences, visit us at www.ReaderService.com/consumerchoice.

HPLP10R

# HARLEQUIN®

## A Romance
## FOR EVERY MOOD™

Spotlight on

## Heart & Home

Heartwarming romances
where love can happen
right when you least expect it.

See the next page to enjoy a sneak peek
from Harlequin Superromance®,
a Heart and Home series.

*Enjoy a sneak peek at fan favorite Molly O'Keefe's*
*Harlequin Superromance miniseries,*
THE NOTORIOUS O'NEILLS, *with*
*TYLER O'NEILL'S REDEMPTION,*
*available September 2010*
*only from Harlequin Superromance.*

Police chief Juliette Tremblant recognized the shape of the man strolling down the street—in as calm and leisurely fashion as if it were the middle of the day rather than midnight. She slowed her car, convinced her eyes were playing tricks on her. It had been a long time since Tyler O'Neill had been seen in this town.

As she pulled to a stop at the curb, he turned toward her, and her heart about stopped.

"What the hell are you doing here, Tyler?"

"Well, if it isn't Juliette Tremblant." He made his way over to her, then leaned down so he could look her in the eye. He was close enough to touch.

Juliette was not, repeat, *not* going to touch Tyler O'Neill. Not with her fingers. Not with a ten-foot pole. There would be no touching. Which was too bad, since it was the only way she was ever going to convince herself the man standing in front of her—as rumpled and heart-stoppingly handsome now as he'd been at sixteen—was real.

And not a figment of all her furious revenge dreams.

"What are you doing back in Bonne Terre?" she asked.

"The manor is sitting empty," Tyler said and shrugged, as though his arriving out of the blue after ten years was casual. "Seems like someone should be watching over the family home."

"You?" She laughed at the very notion of him being here for any unselfish reason. "Please."

He stared at her for a second, then smiled. Her heart fluttered against her chest—a small mechanical bird powered by that smile.

"You're right." But that cryptic comment was all he offered.

Juliette bit her lip against the other questions.

*Why did you go?*

*Why didn't you write? Call?*

*What did I do?*

But what would be the point? Ten years of silence were all the answer she really needed.

She had sworn off feeling anything for this man long ago. Yet one look at him and all the old hurt and rage resurfaced as though they'd been waiting for the chance. That made her mad.

She put the car in gear, determined not to waste another minute thinking about Tyler O'Neill. "Have a good night, Tyler," she said, liking all the cool "go screw yourself" she managed to fit into those words.

*It seems Juliette has an old score to settle with Tyler.*
*Pick up TYLER O'NEILL'S REDEMPTION*
*to see how he makes it up to her.*
*Available September 2010,*
*only from Harlequin Superromance.*

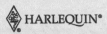
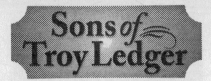

# MARGARET WAY

*introduces*

THE
*Rylance*
DYNASTY

**The lives & loves of
Australia's most powerful family**

Growing up in the spotlight hasn't been easy, but the two
Rylance heirs, Corin and his sister, Zara, have come of age
and are ready to claim their inheritance. Though they are
privileged, proud and powerful, they are about to discover
that there are some things money can't buy....

*Look for:*

# *Australia's Most Eligible Bachelor*

### *Available September*

# *Cattle Baron Needs a Bride*

### *Available October*

**www.eHarlequin.com**

HRI7679